The Rose Beyond the Wall

THE ROSE BEYOND THE WALL

by Kristi D. Holl

Troll Associates

I would like to thank Deb Holl for her help with the medical aspects of this book.

A TROLL BOOK, published by Troll Associates, Mahwah, NJ 07430

Published by arrangement with Atheneum Publishers, a division of Macmillan Publishing Company, Inc. For information address Atheneum Publishers, a division of Macmillan Publishing Company, Inc., 866 Third Avenue, New York, New York 10022.

First Troll Printing, 1988

Printed in the United States of America.

10 9 8 7 6 5 4 3 2 1

ISBN 0-8167-1309-X

Contents

1. *Something's Wrong*
3

2. *Hospice*
18

3. *Getting Ready*
38

4. *Coming Home*
50

5. *Old Friends*
66

6. *Time Out*
73

7. *Gladys*
88

8. *Letting Go*
99

9. *The Rose*
111

10. *Blossom as the Rose*
117

11. *"Be With Me"*
129

12. *The Rose Beyond the Wall*
144

The Rose Beyond the Wall

To my dad,
Delbert Couchman
in loving memory

1

Something's Wrong

ON FRIDAY AFTERNOON, when the doors of Martha Washington Middle School flew open, sixth, seventh, and eighth grade students poured out and flowed down the steps. Although students crushed her toes as they stampeded by, Rachel Lincoln stood just outside the door, searching the crowd for her best friend, Kara Hayes.

When she spotted Kara, she waved wildly. Flowing with the current of students and working her way toward Kara, she called, "What happened to you back there? I thought you were right behind me."

Kara's sheepish smile showed a flash of braces.

"I left my copy of *Kisses in the Sunset* in my locker. I want to finish the book over the weekend."

Rachel ducked her head to cover her grin. Kara devoured every teen romance in their library, and her personality could change with each book. Last week she had read *Wedding Bells for a Southern Belle.* Kara's Deep South accent had been so thick all week that Rachel could barely understand her drawl.

"Can you come with me to Grandma's today?" Rachel asked. "Friday's baking day. I've decided to make her famous German chocolate cake. Grandma always reminds me to invite you."

"I wish I could, especially if you're making cake." Kara licked her lips dreamily. "But I have to baby-sit for Mom today. She volunteers at the day care center on Friday afternoons now." Kara pointed to a group of laughing boys near the chain link fence. "Why not ask Jim? Your grandma loves him."

Rachel studied her childhood friend, Jim Reynolds, as he jostled another boy in his small band. During their growing-up years, Jim had often visited Grandma with her. He probably would enjoy sampling some German chocolate cake. He'd always been a sucker for Grandma's good cooking and baking.

With a grin, she recalled how Grandma's chocolate cake had once enticed a stubborn Jim to marry an eager Rachel. They'd been seven that summer. After playing cowboys and Indians all morning, Rachel had demanded to pick the next game. When Jim agreed, she'd gleefully chosen "bride and groom."

Jim had balked like a mule. *He* wasn't going to play wedding. No way.

Furious, Rachel had jumped on his back, knocking him to the ground. When Grandma had rushed in to see what the commotion was about, Rachel had been whipping Jim with a white bath towel she'd intended to use for a bridal veil.

After separating the wrestling bride and groom, Grandma had promised Jim a real chocolate wedding cake if he'd go through with the ceremony. After a long scowling pause, Jim had agreed, on one condition—that he got to lick the frosting bowl.

Before he could change his mind, Grandma had stepped outside and snipped off a coral-colored rose from her prize-winning bush. Snapping off the thorns, she'd handed it to Rachel. "For your wedding bouquet," she'd said.

Later, a towel-adorned Rachel had lovingly watched Jim devour the miniature chocolate wedding cake. He'd gone back to Grandma P.'s often after that. Rachel bet that his weakness for German chocolate cake hadn't lessened one bit over the last five years.

Rachel twisted her ring around her finger. "I think I *will* ask him to come with me. Jim and I used to do lots of things together, but lately he's always too busy for me."

Kara gawked at Jim through half-shut eyes. "He's so dark and handsome. Just like the hero of *Kisses in the Sunset.*"

"Honestly, Kara. He's just a boy I grew up with. I still have the tooth he knocked out on my back step. That's hardly something to feel romantic about." Waving, she caught Jim's eye and motioned him over.

But when she invited Jim to come with her, he shook his head. "Sorry, Rache. The guys and I have to practice now. It's the only time we can all get together this weekend." He started back to his friends, twirling his drumsticks in the air. "Tell Grandma P. 'hi' for me."

Rachel frowned and pushed her bangs back off her forehead. Jim never seemed to have time for her anymore, and Rachel missed his friendship. They used to do lots of things together, having grown up on the same block and attended the same school.

Disappointed, Rachel walked alone three blocks, then turned down State Street. She and Grandma spent their time together quietly baking or sewing or browsing through old photograph albums. She hoped Grandma wasn't too tired for today's baking lesson. Often during the past weeks, Grandma had been exhausted and cancelled their after school plans.

Her favorite activity with Grandma was sewing. It still gave Rachel a feeling of security. When she had been four years old, Grandma had cared for her for two months while her mom was in the hospital.

She'd taught Rachel how to sew simple doll clothes then. Ever since, sewing had been special. With a needle, a few scraps of material, and her red velvet pin cushion, Grandma worked magic.

One morning when her mother had been in the hospital for several weeks, Rachel had hidden in her closet. Grandma had found her there, clutching a crumpled, yellow dotted Swiss dress her mom had made her for Easter.

Instead of scolding her for wrinkling the dress, Grandma had helped Rachel put it on. Then Grandma hunted in the closet ragbag for leftover scraps of yellow dotted Swiss.

While Rachel had drawn inky faces and colored yellow hair on five wooden clothespins, Grandma cut out and sewed tiny matching dotted Swiss dresses. Using pinking shears, she'd made zigzag hems on all the miniature dresses.

By the time the clothespins were dressed, Rachel had forgotten about being sad. She'd played with her five "twin sisters" the rest of the day.

Rachel still had those clothespin dolls in her top dresser drawer. Wrapped in her old Easter dress, they lay hidden under a lacy slip she'd never worn.

❦

FIFTEEN MINUTES later, Rachel shuffled up the sidewalk in front of Grandma Potter's yellow clapboard house. She let herself inside and waited for her eyes to adjust to the living room's cool, cavelike dimness.

"Grandma! I'm here," she called out, wiping her feet on the rag rug. "I decided on the German chocolate cake for today. Dad's been hinting for one lately."

Rachel baked something new each Friday under Grandma's watchful eye, then took it home for supper. Rachel loved learning to bake, but the best part of these afternoons was having Grandma's undivided attention. Rachel often had a hard time sharing her thoughts with her mother, but she and Grandma operated on the same wavelength.

Rachel hurried through the quiet house. The kitchen was empty. Was Grandma working in the flower beds, or hanging laundry? Rachel looked out the window to the backyard. But her grandmother wasn't there, either.

Suddenly, from the other end of the house, came a faint noise. It sounded like a small gasp or weak cry. Rachel caught her breath sharply.

Grandma!

Rachel raced to the back of the house. She found her grandmother in the bathroom, dragging herself slowly to her feet. Grandma leaned against the wall and clutched her stomach.

"Grandma! Are you all right? Here, let me help you." Rachel put her arm around the older woman and guided her down the hall to the front bedroom. Rachel could feel her grandmother's ribs right through her thin cotton dress.

"I'm sorry you found me like this, honey." Grandma Potter lay back slowly on her bed. "I seem to have come down with the flu. It's going around, you know."

Rachel glanced around the spotless room, from the crocheted doily under the potted philodendron to the faded photograph of the grandfather she hardly remembered.

"I'll go call Mom while you rest. She'll come right over." Rachel started for the door.

"No!" Her grandmother struggled to sit up. "I'm sorry. I meant you don't need to bother her. I'll be just fine."

"It won't be any bother. She'd be upset if I didn't tell her you were sick."

"If I don't feel better tomorrow, I'll call her myself." The blue veins at Grandma's temples bulged. "I promise."

"Then let me make you something to eat—maybe some soup. You could reheat it later when you felt more like eating. How about that?"

Her grandmother opened her violet eyes slowly. "That sounds nice. Maybe you could fix me a cup of tea first."

"Sure, Grandma. Right away." Rachel turned to leave, but paused in the doorway. Lying there, her grandmother looked so frail and thin.

Rachel brewed the tea first and carried it to

Grandma's room. She appeared to be dozing, so she left the tea on the night table and returned to the kitchen.

Quickly Rachel pared two small potatoes. Grandma's favorite soup was potato soup, with lots of butter and thick slices of potatoes. When the potatoes were tender, she left the soup to simmer. Rachel peeked into Grandma's bedroom and was surprised to find her sitting up and sipping her tea.

Grandma carefully lowered the cup to its saucer. "See? I'm better already. Must be a flu bug that comes and goes."

Rachel told her about the potato soup, then fixed her another cup of tea, with the usual two sugar cubes and a piece of dried lemon peel.

Grandma smiled wanly. "I should have had you fix a bowl of snake soup. I haven't had any in a long time."

Rachel laughed. She hadn't thought about snake soup in ages. The summer Grandma had taken care of her, Rachel had learned to make homemade egg noodles. Rachel would get her own ball of egg noodle dough to roll flat and cut into yellow strings.

But no matter how she squished and flattened and sliced, her noodles always turned out fat and slightly misshapen. Rachel had loved to watch Grandma throw them into the bubbling chicken broth. The noodles curled and squirmed just like snakes.

Rachel sat on the edge of the soft bed. "Remember how you let me eat the noodles with my fingers?"

"I remember. You started at the head and ate your way to the tail."

"As long as we were *alone*. Mom would've killed me if she'd seen me eat like that." Rachel held Grandma's hand lightly, stroking it.

After talking about Kara and Jim and school for a while, Rachel sensed that Grandma wanted to sleep. Her lips and cheeks were plaster white.

Giving her a gentle hug, Rachel said, "'Bye, Grandma. I'll call you later."

Her grandmother nodded briefly, then closed her eyes again. Rachel tiptoed out of the house, locking the front door and pulling it closed behind her.

At home, after her mother's last piano student left, Rachel explained about finding Grandma sick. "She seemed tired when I left. She'd had some tea, and I left her some soup to warm up."

Beverly Lincoln combed her fingers through her wispy blonde hair, letting it fall haphazardly back into place. "I just knew I should have visited her today. I'll call her right now."

Rachel consumed two strawberry jam sandwiches while her mom was on the phone. When she hung up, her mother sat with a deep frown creasing her forehead.

"Grandma *said* she's feeling better, but her voice

sounded so breathy." Beverly tapped her fingernail on the counter top. "I'm going to talk to your dad about Grandma as soon as he gets home. I think she should see Dr. Osborne."

When Dad arrived home, he smelled like the juniper trees he'd been pruning at the tree nursery where he worked. The skin around his dark eyes crinkled as he smiled at Rachel.

He bent his six-foot frame over the sink to wash his hands. "How was school, Sunshine?"

"Oh, Dad, I'm too old to be called that." Rachel shook her head at the nickname he'd called her since she was a baby.

"Sorry." His grin didn't make him look sorry at all. "What did you bake at Grandma Potter's for supper tonight?"

Rachel's concern came flooding back at the mention of her grandmother's name. She told him about finding Grandma so sick that afternoon. A few minutes later her older brother, Brent, came home from basketball practice. They continued to discuss Grandma's health during supper.

"Dan, I think Mother needs to see Dr. Osborne," Rachel's mother said. "I've asked her to several times in the past two months, but she always refuses."

Rachel's father salted his hash browns before answering. "I'll visit her after supper tonight. Maybe I can persuade her to go see him."

Rachel relaxed, satisfied that something would get done. Grandma hardly ever refused to do something her dad wanted. Dr. Osborne would prescribe some iron pills or something to pep Grandma up. In no time at all she'd be her old self again.

Rachel and Brent were watching a basketball game on the kitchen TV when her parents returned. Rachel slid down from the high kitchen stool when she glimpsed her mother's troubled expression.

"How's Grandma?" she asked.

"She says she feels fine." Her mother reached for the large bag of corn chips that she always kept in the cupboard. Grabbing a handful of chips, she sank into a chair at the table. "But I don't think she looks very well at all."

Dan Lincoln turned the volume down on the TV. "Grandma thinks it's just the flu, and I'm sure she's right. You worry too much, Beverly. At any rate, you'll know tomorrow after she sees the doctor."

"She agreed to go?" Rachel sighed with relief. "I'll go with you, Mom. What time?"

"Her appointment's at ten-thirty." She crunched through her handful of chips, then went to the cupboard for more. "I'll be glad to have your company."

Rachel turned back to watch the end of the game. Everything would be fine after tomorrow, she thought. In fact, maybe tomorrow afternoon Grandma could show her how to make that German chocolate cake.

The next morning they arrived ten minutes early at the family practice clinic where Dr. Osborne saw his patients. Rachel was surprised Grandma had received an appointment so fast. Maybe the doctor gave older people special privileges.

While waiting, Rachel thumbed through a tattered, out-of-date *Parents* magazine.

Her grandmother sat quietly, fiddling with the clasp on the purse she clutched. She jumped slightly when the nurse glided into the waiting room and called her name.

Beverly leaned forward. "Do you want me to come in with you, Mother?"

"Heavens, no!" Grandma Potter smiled to soften the words. "I can get in there under my own steam, thank you."

Rachel grinned behind her magazine. Grandma sounded perfectly fine now. They probably all worried too much.

She squirmed around in her plastic chair, trying to find something to read. It was difficult deciding between "Potty Trained in 24 Hours!" and "Make Sibling Rivalry Obsolete."

Twenty minutes later, after learning how not to rival her older sibling, Rachel gradually became aware of angry voices. The words grew louder and more distinct. They seemed to come from Dr. Osborne's office.

Suddenly, Rachel realized the angry voice belonged to Grandma. She was *yelling* at the doctor.

"Oh, no, I *won't*! And that's final!"

Rachel whirled in her seat. At that moment, Grandma threw open Dr. Osborne's door with a bang. Her cheeks were flushed, and her violet eyes snapped. "If you can't diagnose better than that, maybe you'd better find another profession!"

Rachel gasped. Grandma and Dr. Osborne had been close friends for years. He had delivered Grandma's only child. Then, many years later, he had comforted Grandma when her husband had died from a heart attack.

Rachel couldn't imagine what Dr. Osborne had said to make Grandma actually yell at him!

With quiet dignity, Grandma turned her back to the doctor. "I'm going out to the car now. Are you two coming?"

"In . . . in a minute, Mother," Beverly stammered. "I want to talk to the doctor for a moment."

Grandma glared briefly at the doctor. Then, her back ramrod stiff, she marched out the door.

Dr. Osborne ran bony fingers through his bushy hair. His white coat, unbuttoned as usual, hung limply on his tall thin frame.

"What in the world did you say to Mother?" Rachel's mom asked.

"Come into the office a minute, Beverly. You, too, Rachel," the doctor said. "We need to talk about something."

Rachel followed her mother into the office and

stood behind her chair. Dr. Osborne perched on the edge of his cluttered desk.

"I'm going to need your help, both of you." Dr. Osborne pulled at his bottom lip. "Minna has convinced herself she's perfectly healthy, but I'm afraid she hasn't been well for some time."

"What's the matter with Grandma?" Rachel blurted out.

"I don't know for sure. I want her to check into the hospital for a couple of days so I can run some tests. But she insists she's healthy as a horse and won't consider it."

Rachel's mother yanked on a loose thread on her cuff. "What exactly would you be testing her for?"

Dr. Osborne scratched his head again. As she studied the somber look on the doctor's face, an icy chill ran down Rachel's neck.

"Several symptoms have me concerned. She's lost some weight since her last checkup and is becoming dehydrated."

"What's that?" Rachel interrupted.

"She's losing too much water from her system. This could be from her vomiting yesterday, and probably is." Dr. Osborne paused, his bushy eyebrows drawn together over his long nose. "But I also noticed her abdomen is rounded, in spite of losing quite a bit of weight. There's some kind of growth there—a tumor."

"Oh, no!" Rachel's mother lurched forward, her hand at her throat. "Cancer?"

"Not necessarily! Not at all," the doctor assured them quickly. "But you can see why I want Minna in the hospital for tests. We need to find out what the growth is."

"I've been so worried about Mother lately. I should have known there was something wrong." Rachel's mother slumped in the chair. "I just don't know how we'll get her to the hospital. She fought just coming to your office."

"Convince her somehow, Beverly. It's important to get these tests done immediately." His voice was unusually brisk, no nonsense. "I want her in the hospital Monday morning."

Rachel stared at the floor as the room seemed to tilt. Grandma couldn't be *that* sick! But the doctor said she needed those tests, and soon. He hadn't said it in so many words, but it sounded like a matter of life or death.

She looked directly at Dr. Osborne and the room slowly stopped spinning. "Reserve a room for Grandma at the hospital on Monday. We'll get her there. I promise."

Hospice

THE NEXT AFTERNOON, while her parents read the Sunday newspaper, Rachel walked over to her grandmother's house. The day before, all her mother's arguing could only persuade Grandma to *think* about taking those tests. Rachel had barely slept at all the night before. She just had to convince Grandma to check into the hospital.

She found Grandma Potter in her front room, surrounded by old photograph albums. She cradled a discolored picture taken when she and Grandpa Potter were first married. The photo's brown edges curled slightly.

Rachel perched on the arm of the couch. "Do you like looking at pictures of Grandpa? Doesn't it make you sad?"

"Oh, no, not at all," Grandma replied. "It triggers happy memories. I especially treasure the pictures of when your mother was a little girl."

Rachel peered closer at the young, bearded man in the picture. "Sometimes I forget what Grandpa looked like."

"This probably sounds terrible, but every once in a while my mind gets hazy too. Then I can't picture him either." Grandma leaned back and removed her reading glasses. "But I never have trouble remembering what a kind and gentle man he was."

Rachel had a sudden idea. "If Grandpa were alive today, do you think he'd want you to have those tests done on Monday?"

Grandma studied Rachel carefully. "Yes, I guess he would want me to."

"Why would he want that?"

Grandma traced his face in the old picture. "Because he loved me," she said softly. "And he worried about me."

"We worry about you too, Grandma."

Grandma laughed suddenly. "I guess you think you've cornered me, don't you, young lady?" She paused, then sighed deeply. "I'll have those tests, but not because I think I'm sick. I just don't want you to worry."

"Thanks, Grandma. Mom will be so glad." Rachel had heard her mother pacing up and down the hall until two A.M. "Mom may not say much, but she's really worried too. In fact, she's eaten two whole family-size bags of corn chips since Friday, just thinking about you."

Grandma laughed out loud. "I know how she eats when she's upset. She always has, ever since she was little. Two whole bags? I guess she really does care a lot!"

Rachel grinned, glad that they understood each other. She inched over near her to enjoy the rest of the pictures. It was comforting to sit close, smelling the violet cologne on the handkerchief tucked in Grandma's belt.

They pored over the pictures for another hour, and neither of them mentioned the tests again.

School on Monday dragged on seemingly without end. Rachel watched the clock constantly, urging the hands to move faster. She knew Grandma was to begin her tests that morning. She might even have some minor surgery to determine what the lump in her stomach was. A *biopsy*, her mother had called it.

Rachel was glad she had art Monday afternoons. She loved art—firing pottery, creating collages and murals, designing mosaics. At home she had even turned one corner of her bedroom into a "studio." There she painted, or polished rocks or made new barrettes from stones and seashells she'd collected. She became totally absorbed in whatever she was making. She hoped today it would take her mind off what was happening at the hospital.

But Rachel discovered that weaving on Miss Scott's big loom didn't take much concentration. She worked smoothly, pushing and pulling the shuttle back and forth, but it left her a lot of time to think.

When the dismissal bell rang, Rachel grabbed her school books and dashed for the door. After dumping them in her locker, she raced home, barely waving good-bye to Kara.

As she turned onto Jefferson Street, she spotted her mother driving down the block from the other direction. Rachel jogged the rest of the way, meeting their blue compact car as it swung into the driveway.

"How's Grandma?" Rachel called through the unopened car window. "What did the tests show?"

Her mother crawled out of the front seat, as if every movement caused excruciating pain. The expression on her mother's face could only mean one thing: bad news.

"Come in the house where we can talk," her mother said, plodding up the back steps. She seemed to have aged ten years overnight. Her shoulders stooped, she unlocked the back door.

"What happened? How *is* Grandma?"

"Sit down at the table," her mother directed.

"I'll make us some hot chocolate." She shuffled around the kitchen in slow motion, heating the milk in the microwave, then adding cocoa and sugar. Carrying two cups, she joined Rachel at the table.

"Have you been at the hospital all this time?" Rachel asked.

"Yes." Her mother gripped her cup of hot chocolate with both hands, as if needing its warmth. "Grandma's finally resting. Dr. Osborne gave her something to help her sleep."

Rachel waited in silence, sensing her mother was groping for words. The ticking of the wall clock and the clink of the refrigerator's ice-maker were the only sounds in the silent kitchen.

"Dr. Osborne did the tests this morning. The biopsy only took a short time." Her hand jerked, and cocoa sloshed over the side of the cup. "The lump was malignant."

"Does that mean cancer?"

Her mother nodded. "Dr. Osborne did the biopsy early this morning. The results were back quickly."

"How did Grandma take the news?" Rachel was astounded at the matter-of-fact tone of her voice, considering the knot in her stomach.

"At first she insisted the X rays were mixed up. She refused to believe they were hers." Her mother mopped up the puddle of cocoa on the table. "Then she argued with the doctor, saying the pathology report couldn't possibly be back so soon. She was convinced the report was meant for another patient."

Rachel frowned. "That doesn't sound like Grandma. She hardly ever argues with anybody."

"Well, she did this morning. Dr. Osborne wanted to remove the tumor right away. He was afraid that if he allowed Grandma to go home, she'd never come back for the surgery. He was probably right. She can be so stubborn."

Rachel tasted her cooling hot chocolate. "It sounds like she was just scared to me."

Her mother reached for the corn chips. "I suppose you're right. I guess that wasn't a very nice comment to make. It's been a trying day."

"But she did finally agree?"

"Yes. So Dr. Osborne removed the lump this afternoon. Then Grandma was in recovery another two hours before I could see her." She pushed back her hair with a shaking hand. "Oh, Rachel, she looked so tiny in that big hospital bed!"

Rachel awkwardly patted her mother's arm, trying to take it all in. *Cancer!* It just couldn't be true!

"Did you talk to Grandma?" she finally asked.

"For a few minutes. She was so groggy, though—I don't think she knew I was there." She popped two more chips into her mouth. "I wanted to break the news to you in person, but I need to go back to the hospital now. The nurse said I could talk to Dr. Osborne when he made rounds at four-thirty."

"I'll come too." Rachel dumped her cooled cocoa in the sink. "I'll wait in the lobby while you see Grandma. Then you can tell me what Dr. Osborne says as soon as you see him."

"Okay, honey. Let me call your dad at the nursery first. I haven't even had a chance to tell him yet."

While her mother used the telephone, Rachel slipped into her jacket. She had to keep reminding herself that this wasn't some nightmare she'd magically awaken from. Nothing seemed real to her. She felt as if she could run over to Grandma's house, just like always, and find her in the kitchen baking bread or in the garden weeding her strawberries.

Mentally shaking herself, she tied her jogging shoes and grabbed her sketch pad. She'd draw while she waited in the lobby.

When they pulled into the Ashmore Community Hospital fifteen minutes later, her mother pointed to a window at the end of the wing. "That's Grandma's room—the one with the blue flowered curtains. She was lucky to get a first floor room. When she's feeling better, she can watch people going by."

Boring, Rachel thought to herself. Surely when Grandma was feeling better, she could simply come home.

Inside the cool, bustling lobby, Rachel curled up in the corner of an orange vinyl-covered couch. Balancing her sketch pad on her knees, she watched her mother disappear around the end of the corridor.

A glass cooler, half filled with fresh flower arrangements, occupied one corner of the lobby. The low table in front of her held a meager selection of the usual out-of-date magazines, some missing their covers. A drinking fountain opposite was flanked by two pay phones.

Examining the carnations and mums in the cooler, Rachel had an idea. She wasn't old enough to visit Grandma in person—hospital rules—but nothing prevented her from waving through the window. Hunched over her sketch pad, she drew with quick, sure strokes.

Twenty minutes later, she finished the border around a picture of a giant bouquet of carnations and roses. In bold scarlet letters across the top, she wrote GET WELL SOON, GRANDMA! She hoped the lettering was dark enough for Grandma to see through the window.

Outside, she sauntered nonchalantly down the sidewalk near the building. Pausing in front of the window with the blue flowered curtains, she glanced over her shoulder. No one appeared to notice her. Inching close to the glass, she peered in.

Shadowy figures moved across her field of vision. Leaning closer, Rachel recognized the back of her mother's head as she leaned over a bed. All she could see of Grandma Potter was the long mound her legs made under the blanket.

Rachel tapped on the window. Inside, no one moved. She tapped a little louder. Her mother whirled around and blinked.

Fearful of being discovered by a nurse, Rachel quickly held up her sketch pad and pressed the picture against the window. Her mother smiled suddenly, then moved aside for Grandma to see.

Hand flat against the window, Rachel waved slightly and pressed her nose against the glass. The orange setting sun behind her reflected brightly in the window. She cupped her hands around her eyes to cut the glare.

Rachel gasped when she saw her grandmother. Her pallor nearly matched the sheets on the bed, and her neatly curled hair was squashed and matted. Her false teeth had been removed, and her face looked caved in.

Forcing a stiff smile, Rachel waved again. Grandma lifted her hand slowly, but it fell back weakly onto the bedspread.

Rachel carefully mouthed the words "I love you," then stepped back from the window. Returning to the lobby, she brushed her hand across her eyes.

After flipping through several health magazines, Rachel spotted her mother and Dr. Osborne coming through the double glass doors. She jumped up, scraping her shin on the table.

"Mom! How's Grandma?" Rachel rushed up to them. "Hi, Dr. Osborne."

"Dr. Osborne was just about to tell me. When I mentioned that you were waiting, he said he'd come out with me." She smiled gratefully at the tall, lanky doctor.

"Let's sit down." Dr. Osborne folded himself down into a chair in one corner.

"Is Grandma all right?" Rachel demanded immediately. "When can we take her home?"

Dr. Osborne ruffled his hair until it resembled a bush badly in need of pruning. "Minna needs to recuperate in the hospital before she can go home. But her general health is good, and she's stubborn in a good kind of way. She won't lie around here any longer than she has to."

Rachel's mother stared at her lap, polishing and repolishing her sunglasses. "Can you tell us how the surgery went? Did you get all the tumor?"

The doctor linked his long fingers together and seemed to inspect his ten square nails. "I got most of it, Beverly. But I couldn't get it all." He looked up, and there was pain in his kind eyes. "I removed enough so that Minna should be comfortable."

"Comfortable?" Rachel tried to keep her voice even, but it rose shrilly. "What do you mean? If you didn't remove all the cancer, won't it keep spreading?"

"I wish I could deny that. I *can* say that for a month or more, Minna may feel like her old self." He put his fingertips together, forming a peak. "But yes, the cancer will grow again."

Rachel's mother grabbed Dr. Osborne's immaculate sleeve. "No, that can't be true!"

"I'm so sorry, Beverly, I really am. But she waited too long to see me. The tumor had grown and spread too far to remove it all." Dr. Osborne took Rachel's and Beverly's hands and gripped them tightly. "I wish I could have done more."

Rachel took a deep breath. "Is . . . is Grandma going to die?"

"Maybe not for a long time." The doctor's shoulders drooped and he spread his hands wide. "I've seen patients last for many months longer than I expected. This disease *can* go into remission—or stop growing—for months. There's just no telling."

"Can you do anything else for her?" Rachel's mother asked. "Would more surgery help?"

"Probably not, but hopefully some chemotherapy will destroy the cancer that's left." He patted Rachel's mother on the shoulder. "I don't want to raise your hopes too much, but you know we'll do everything we possibly can."

"I know." Rachel's mother's voice sounded hollow. "Thank you for coming out and talking to us."

After Dr. Osborne left, Rachel went to sit on the arm of her mother's chair. "Do you want me to call Dad?"

"No, honey, but thanks." Her mother searched her purse for her car keys. "I'm fine. Let's go home."

Arm in arm, they walked slowly to the car, and drove home in silence.

The next few days seemed hazy and unfocused to Rachel. Her parents insisted that she go to school, but she couldn't concentrate. So she daydreamed and doodled sketches of "get well" cards on the corners of her papers. After school each day, Rachel caught the city bus for the hospital, armed with a bright new picture for Grandma. Her mother spent every afternoon there, so they rode home together.

By the end of the week, the I.V. bags were gone. Grandma was able to sit up, eat some fruit and awful-looking molded green Jello, and watch TV. She began to wave cheerily at Rachel through the window.

In spite of Dr. Osborne's warning, Rachel's hope soared. Grandma looked healthier every day. She wasn't going to die! Like all doctors, Dr. Osborne had just been overly gloomy.

In no time at all, Grandma would come home. Rachel was sure of it.

Over the weekend, Rachel's mom was surprised to receive a phone call from a nurse named Marcia Carlson. She wanted to stop and talk to the whole family.

Monday evening, a week after Grandma's surgery, the doorbell rang. On the top step stood a young woman, tall and slim, with a professional air about her. Rachel had expected someone in a starched nurse's uniform. Instead the visitor wore casual slacks, and her straight dark hair was held back by large barrettes.

"Hello. I'm Marcia Carlson. Are your parents home?"

"Yes. Come in." Suddenly tongue-tied, Rachel led the way to the living room, where her parents and Brent waited.

Rachel studied Nurse Carlson as introductions were made. Then Miss Carlson explained why she had called. She was part of a volunteer program to help terminally ill patients and their families.

Terminally ill! Rachel *hated* that phrase. It sounded cold and clinical. It couldn't possibly apply to Grandma.

Her ears perked up at Marcia Carlson's next words. "You know the seriousness of Mrs. Potter's condition. I've visited with her often, and she is fully aware of it herself."

"I didn't know that," Rachel's mother said. "Mother never mentioned it to me."

"When I talked with Mrs. Potter last week, we discussed many things." Marcia Carlson pushed her long hair back over her shoulder. "Mrs. Lincoln, your mother would like to come home."

Come home? Rachel clapped her hands together.

Dr. Osborne *had* been wrong! Grandma was going to be fine. The nurse had just said she could come home!

"I don't think I understand." Beverly Lincoln stared at the nurse for a minute, frowning. "Is she strong enough to come home?"

Rachel's father leaned forward, his arms hanging loosely between his knees. "We were under the impression that she would—what I mean is—that she'd be living the time she has left in the hospital. Dr. Osborne said chemotherapy would be started soon."

"True. But that can be done on an out-patient basis. You could bring her to the hospital for the treatments, which take only an hour or so, and then take her home again." Miss Carlson smiled warmly.

Rachel's mother suddenly stopped twisting her wedding band and smiled. "Mother is a lot better than Dr. Osborne thought, isn't she? She must be, if she can come home."

Nurse Carlson's smile drained away. "I'm so sorry. I thought you understood. I didn't mean to raise any false hopes."

Rachel's stomach lurched, feeling just like the time she plunged down the state fair's double loop roller coaster ride.

"Mrs. Potter doesn't want to spend the rest of her time in the hospital. She wants to die at home, among her family."

Rachel slumped in her chair at the full impact of

the nurse's words, which, in the silence of the room, seemed to fall like glass marbles.

Brent spoke for the first time. "How could we manage? We aren't set up like a hospital here, and none of us has any medical training."

"That's where I fit in. I'll check on Mrs. Potter once a week, or as often as you need me. Dr. Osborne and I will be in contact frequently about her condition."

"Even so . . ." Rachel's dad said. His voice trailed off, full of doubt.

"I would instruct you in what foods she could eat, and what to expect as her illness progresses." Nurse Carlson studied each family member in turn. "Doctors are beginning to recognize the importance of patients living these last months at home. Terminally ill people often want to be with people they love, in familiar surroundings."

Rachel's mother spoke timidly, as if afraid of the nurse's reaction. "I'm not sure I could take care of her properly."

"I'd help!" Rachel cried.

"I know you would." Her mother hesitated, then rushed on. "I don't think I could watch my own mother die!"

Marcia Carlson nodded sympathetically. "It's perfectly normal to feel that way. Please understand that this isn't something you have to do."

"Yes, we do. If my mother wants to leave the hospital, how could we refuse?"

Nurse Carlson went to sit by Rachel's mother on the couch. "There is one alternative. We're lucky here. Our county has an active hospice program, in which many doctors and nurses voluntarily provide home care for terminally ill patients."

"What's a hospice program?" Rachel asked.

"Our hospice program is an independent, non-profit organization. We serve terminally ill patients and their families in our area. Those of us in the program feel strongly that a patient has the right to die at home."

Brent turned from the window where he had been standing. "But you mentioned an alternative to having Grandma live here?"

The nurse nodded. "There are places in the county—one just a few miles from here—that are hospice homes. These homes are supported by private donations. They're set up for people who want to spend their final months in a homey atmosphere, but who don't have relatives who are able to care for them."

"Grandma could go to one of these homes?"

Rachel was shocked to hear relief in Brent's voice. She spoke angrily. "We won't let Grandma go there. She'll come live with us, won't she, Mom?"

Before Rachel's mother could answer, Brent interrupted. "If we just think about this, we'll see it won't work. Mom's piano students come in and out at all hours, and Grandma might not appreciate all that noisy banging."

"I could give up my piano students, at least for a while."

"But you're not a nurse, Mom! Do you want to be tied down to the house every waking minute? You'd have to give up all those Garden Club and committee meetings."

"Somehow, that doesn't sound like much of a sacrifice."

The nurse broke in smoothly by handing Rachel's parents a sheaf of papers. "This is a private decision, too big to make right away. Please read this brochure and the other information, then we'll talk again soon."

Rachel's mother waved her hand helplessly at the papers. "Oh, Dan, I just don't know. I can't seem to think straight tonight."

Marcia Carlson opened another manilla folder. "When you consider whether or not to have Mrs. Potter come home to live with you, you'll need to discuss many things."

"Like what?" Rachel asked, still glaring at Brent.

"First, your brother raised some good questions. As a family, you need to decide if you can provide the kind of environment that your grandmother will need at this point."

Rachel's mother reached for the untouched coffee pot on the tray. "What do you mean, environment?" She slowly poured three cups of coffee.

"For instance, will there be a separate room for her? Will someone be here at all times, in case she needs anything?" She paused and sipped at her coffee. "Can you stand to see her in pain? She won't feel well sometimes, especially right after her chemotherapy treatments."

Beverly Lincoln clutched her warm mug as if it were a life ring. "There *is* a lot to think about, isn't there?"

Nurse Carlson nodded. "The last big question is perhaps the hardest to answer. Will your family be able to handle the pressure this situation will bring?"

"I don't know. We'd like to think so." Rachel's father set down his full cup of coffee. "When do you need our decision?"

"She won't be ready to leave the hospital for another week or so. But to arrange a room for her at the hospice home nearby, we'd need to know within the next three days, if possible."

Rachel's father stood and paced back and forth across the room. "I do have one reservation. I think Grandma *should* come live with us. But when the . . . end . . . is near, I think she should be in the hospital where the doctors can make her comfortable."

"That is something else to consider. First, let me

give you our feelings on the matter," the nurse said. "Except when absolutely necessary, we don't like to transfer hospice patients to the hospital. At a very stressful time, it's asking them to make a difficult adjustment to frightening surroundings."

"But I don't want Mother in pain," Beverly Lincoln insisted.

"We agree. We don't hesitate to give sufficient medication for relief of pain. *Comfort* is our main concern." Nurse Carlson reached for her sweater and purse. "I'll go now. I've given you so much to talk about, and I know how difficult this is for you. Call me in a few days."

After she left, Rachel's family sat in stunned silence for several minutes.

Her father finally spoke. "Let's all go to bed now. It's getting late." He stood and stretched. "We'll discuss this tomorrow. It will have to be a family decision."

Wide-eyed, Rachel tossed throughout the night. She watched the lighted dial on her clock as the hands passed three o'clock, then four o'clock.

She compared Grandma's sterile hospital room to the homey atmosphere she was used to living in. They just *had* to bring Grandma home to live with them where they could take good care of her. Call it instinct or just a prediction, but Rachel knew that if Grandma came home, she would amaze Dr. Osborne and get well. Hugging that belief close, she finally fell into a fitful sleep.

Rachel's family talked of little the next few days except Nurse Carlson's words. Rachel and her mother wanted Grandma brought home right away. Rachel's father did too, although he wondered if they really knew what they were attempting. But Rachel's mom assured him that she could handle it.

They planned to convert the enclosed porch on the back of the house into an extra bedroom. With some of Grandma's familiar things brought over from her house, it would seem more like home to her.

On Friday, Rachel stood near the phone as her father placed the call. "Nurse Carlson? This is Dan Lincoln, Minna Potter's son-in-law." He paused and listened for a moment. "Yes, we've reached a decision. When can she be released?"

He hung up the phone and turned around. Rachel smiled and wrapped her arms around his waist. "Grandma belongs with us. I'm glad she's coming home."

3

Getting Ready

ON HER WAY down to breakfast the next morning, Rachel stopped at the door of Brent's room. He was lifting weights, as he did nearly every morning.

"Can I talk to you a minute?" she asked, plopping down on his unmade bed.

"Sure, Squirt." Brent clenched his jaw and slowly straightened his arms overhead, until he held the barbell high. "What about?"

"Grandma." Rachel pulled her knees up to her chest and wrapped her arms around them. "Do you know very much about cancer?"

"No, but I think it's real common, at least in old

people." His biceps glistened with sweat as he slowly lowered the barbell.

"Do you think Grandma's going to die?"

"What kind of question is that?" Brent wiped his face with a dingy gray towel. "After an operation like Grandma's, the cancer can stop growing for years."

Rachel picked at the fuschia polish on her toenails. "That doesn't sound like what the nurse said."

"You must have misunderstood her. I have to get dressed now, so do you mind?"

Rachel padded barefooted to the door, then turned. "I think the nurse said Grandma wanted to come home to die." Her voice was barely more than a whisper.

"Look," Brent snapped. "What good is it to talk about it? It's a depressing topic."

Shoulders slumped, Rachel plodded down the stairs. She could hear her parents in the kitchen. Rachel was glad her dad had stayed home late on this Saturday morning. She had a lot of questions she wanted to ask them.

However, when she walked into the kitchen, her parents stopped talking in mid-sentence.

Rachel shivered in the uncomfortable silence. "What's for breakfast?" she asked, although she wasn't at all hungry.

With obvious relief, Rachel's mother opened the refrigerator door. "Would you like scrambled eggs? Or an omelet with cheese? Maybe a bagel."

"The bagel, I guess. Are there any raisin ones?" Rachel got her juice glass from the cupboard.

She didn't quite know how to phrase her question. She groped for the right words, then took a deep breath and plunged in.

"How will Grandma be when she comes home?" She poured Cranapple juice into her glass.

Rachel intercepted the wary glance that passed between her parents before her mother replied. "Well, Grandma will be weak from the surgery, of course. She'll want to nap a lot at first."

"But what about later? You know, when the tumor grows back? Will she seem the same?" Rachel blurted her questions, relieved at last to get them out in the open.

Her mother scrubbed the spotless stove, her back to Rachel. "She will be just the same," she finally said.

Rachel blinked in surprise. How could Grandma be dying, but act just the same? She turned to her father, but he avoided her look and gazed out the window.

Rachel tried once more. "What should we talk to her about? We can't pretend that nothing's happened."

"Of course not." Her father shoved his hands into his pockets. "But Grandma has many years left. We'll be glad to have her living with us, but there's no need for anything to change."

Rachel nodded, pretending to understand. She buttered her raisin bagel and carried it to the table.

Had she misunderstood Dr. Osborne's and the nurse's words? Brent and her parents seemed to think Grandma would be fine for a long time, once she fully recovered from the surgery.

She'd love to believe that, but it didn't coincide with what she remembered. Her bagel sat like a hard rock in her stomach. She had a strong suspicion that her parents were keeping things from her because they felt she couldn't handle the truth.

After a silent breakfast, Rachel took some agates and quartz to polish out on the front porch. Chin resting in her hands, she studied Jim's house half a block away, wishing he would appear soon.

Jim knew how she felt about Grandma. *He* would understand her fears.

Twenty minutes later she spotted Jim coming through the bridal wreath hedge that bordered his house. Hunched over the dented handle bars, he steered his wobbly bike in her direction.

Rachel jogged to the street curb and waved. Jim braked, coasting to a stop in front of her.

"Hi, Jim!" She balanced on the edge of the cement curb. "Got a minute?"

"Sure. What's up?" Jim brushed his unruly black hair out of his eyes.

"Grandma's coming home pretty soon. She's

going to live with us." Rachel peered up at Jim, shading her eyes against the sun's bright glare.

"She'll love that, at least until she's strong enough to go home again. Can't wait to taste some of Grandma P.'s lemon meringue pie." He smacked his lips loudly.

"I don't think she'll ever go home again." Rachel forced the words out. "Both Dr. Osborne and a nurse told us she wants to die at home."

Jim whistled low, then propped his bike against a tree. He sat down on the curb beside Rachel. "You mean the surgery didn't work?"

"Dr. Osborne got most of the tumor, but not all. Sooner or later, it'll grow back."

Jim hesitated, then reached over and patted Rachel's arm. "I'm sorry, Rache."

"Me, too. Only you know something? It doesn't seem real. Grandma looks better every day." Rachel scratched a mosquito bite on the back of her neck. "Mom and Dad and Brent think she's going to live for years."

"What do you think?"

"I don't know." Rachel picked up a handful of gravel from the gutter. "I'd like to believe them, but I don't feel like Mom and Dad are telling me the whole truth."

Jim knotted a broken shoelace, then stood up. "Parents do that. They think they have to protect us."

He wheeled his bike back into the street. "But who knows? They could be right about Grandma P."

"After I see Grandma this morning, do you want to do something? We haven't done anything on a Saturday for a long time." Rachel poured the sandy gravel from one hand to the other.

Jim wiggled his loose kick stand with his foot. "I wish I could, Rache. But I promised Ted that I'd go with him to that new science fiction movie at the Strand."

"Oh." Rachel's shoulders sagged, then she brightened. "I could come with you! We haven't seen a Saturday afternoon movie for ages!"

"Um, well, maybe not this time," he stammered. He fiddled with his loose bike chain, then blurted out, "It's like this. I think we might meet Suzanne and Kathy there. Maybe."

Rachel felt her face grow warm. Jim and Ted were meeting *girls* at the movies? She wouldn't let Jim see, but that hurt. She and Jim used to go to the Saturday matinees together. Suddenly he seemed more interested in Suzanne and Kathy.

"Sure. Maybe another time. I don't butt in where I'm not wanted." She stood and brushed the grass off her jeans.

"Hey, that's not it, Rache. You and I are *friends*. But I have other friends too." Jim kicked at his half-flat front tire.

"Fine." Rachel pivoted on her heel and stalked up the front walk. "I just remembered something I have to do this afternoon anyway. I'll be too busy to watch some dumb movie." She flounced up the steps and through the door, letting the screen door slam shut behind her.

Rachel fumed as she took the stairs two at a time. She just didn't understand Jim! They'd been best friends—blood brothers, even—since first grade. But this year he had no time for her. He was either too busy with his drumsticks or his baseball. *Now* he'd sprouted an interest in *girls*. Rachel pounded the bannister angrily. She'd always thought she could count on him.

Rachel finally erased Jim from her mind that afternoon as she helped her mother. They could have used a bulldozer to clean out the junk on the enclosed porch at the back of the house. Empty and stripped of its grimy blinds, it was a nice, sunny room, perfect for a bedroom for Grandma.

Rachel knew she'd love it. There was a clear view of her mother's formal rose garden near the back fence. Or Grandma could study the wrens and chickadees that flocked around the bird feeders. The room was quiet, facing away from the street. A good place to recuperate.

On Sunday afternoon Rachel and her parents went to Grandma's house to collect a few of her things. While her parents packed Grandma's clothes, Rachel wandered through the deserted rooms. Without Grandma, the small house seemed larger than before, and it echoed.

Walking past the brown tweed couch, Rachel kicked over Grandma's sewing basket. She stooped to gather the variegated balls of yarn that rolled under the couch.

Part of a crocheted afghan lay in the bottom of the wicker basket. Rachel set Grandma's sewing by the front door to take home. Maybe, after resting a while, Grandma would feel like finishing it.

In the bedroom Rachel watched her mother pack Grandma's warmest flannel nightgowns. Her dad rummaged in the closet, emerging with pale blue house slippers and some black low-heeled shoes.

Rachel was confident they would get everything Grandma *needed*. She intended to also include things to make Grandma feel at home.

"Mom, can I get some of Grandma's books?" Rachel knelt by the book rack next to the bed.

"That would be nice, honey," her mother said absent-mindedly.

Rachel ran her finger along the book spines, then picked up a volume of poetry. Inside, the edges of the pages were worn thin, as if they'd been turned a million times. Closing it, she reached for the two padded velvet photograph albums in the pile. She leafed through the old pictures quickly.

"Ready to go, Rachel?" Her father resembled a

clothes rack with Grandma's sweaters and house coat draped over his arm. "I think we have everything."

"Just a minute."

Rachel closed the albums, gripped them under one arm, then clutched Grandma's old Bible and the book of poems under the other arm. She shuffled toward the door, past the dresser where her grandfather's picture sat. Shifting her books, Rachel added the photo to her load. It would look just right on the night table in Grandma's new bedroom.

The next few days passed quickly for Rachel as she helped fix up the porch in the evenings. Gradually, with the addition of ruffly yellow gingham curtains and a yellow bedspread, it looked more like a bedroom.

Finally, with her grandfather's sober picture on the night table beside Grandma's books, Rachel was satisfied. It was a perfect room for Grandma to get well in.

On Wednesday evening Rachel was coming downstairs just as the doorbell rang. She glimpsed Marcia Carlson standing on the doorstep. Rachel scrambled back up the stairs, a twist of fear in her stomach.

What was that nurse doing here again? Was Grandma worse? Couldn't she come home after all?

Rachel listened over the bannister as Miss Carlson was led into the living room. She padded silently down the stairs again, staying out of sight in the hallway.

"Mrs. Lincoln, your mother is coming along better than we'd expected. I think she'll be ready to come home Friday. How does that sound to you?"

"Great!" Rachel burst into the room. "We've fixed up the porch for Grandma already, with her favorite things in it."

The nurse smiled warmly, unruffled by Rachel's sudden appearance. "I'm glad to hear that. Your grandmother is anxious to leave the hospital." She looked from Brent to Rachel to her parents. "I wanted to make sure you all feel this is the best thing."

One by one, with Brent last, Rachel's family nodded their agreement. Her mother spoke for them all. "Grandma belongs with us."

"I'm so glad to hear that. I came tonight to prepare you for when she comes home."

Avoiding her parents' eyes, Rachel asked, "What will Grandma be like when she comes home?"

"Weak, at first. After being in bed so long at the hospital, coming home on Friday will tire her out." Nurse Carlson's voice was soothing and professional. "She'll be bedridden for a while, but as she regains her strength she'll probably want to move about the house more."

Rachel's father, who hadn't visited the hospital for several days, asked, "How does Grandma look now?"

"She's still pale, but that's expected. She's lost a little more weight from being on a liquid diet." Marcia

Carlson grinned suddenly. "But she's a fighter, looking very well for what she's been through the last two weeks."

"She's a fighter?" Rachel's father asked. "Do you mean she's given the hospital staff some trouble?"

"Nothing unusual. She thinks the nurses bother her too much. She doesn't think Dr. Osborne knows what tests to order or what diet to prescribe. But this anger is perfectly normal."

"Diet?" Rachel's mother twisted her hands together in her lap. "How will I know what food to fix? Is she on a special diet?"

The nurse handed Rachel's mother a typed list of the foods allowed on Grandma's diet. She explained how the diet would gradually change, from all liquids to soft foods like poached eggs, ground meat, and mashed potatoes.

Nurse Carlson assured them she'd come at least once a week to check on Grandma, and more often if they wanted her to.

"I'll come Friday when Mrs. Potter is brought home," she said. "I'll stay until she's comfortably settled in."

"Thank you." Rachel's mother extended her hand. "You've already helped so much. I'm glad you're only a phone call away."

"Please feel free to call me any time. The hospice volunteers do care for patients, but we're just as concerned about the patient's family."

She shook hands with Rachel's parents and nodded at Brent. Rachel walked with her to the door.

Rachel studied the young nurse, curious about something. "Can I ask you something?" Marcia nodded. "Why do you work with dying people? You don't even get paid for it, do you?"

The young woman leaned against the doorway. "It's true I don't get any money for this, but I do feel rewarded."

"How?"

"Death is the final act in anyone's life, and it can be very frightening." The nurse touched Rachel's shoulder. "I have a special opportunity to comfort the dying patient and to help the family members. It may not sound like it, but it *is* rewarding."

Rachel leaned against the screen door as Marcia Carlson got into her beat-up old car and rattled off down the street.

She liked Nurse Carlson. She was kind, but honest. She didn't hide the truth, acting as if Rachel were too young to handle it.

Rachel nodded to herself. Marcia Carlson was going to be a good friend.

4

Coming Home

LATE FRIDAY AFTERNOON Rachel rearranged Grandma's night table four times before she heard the family car pull into the driveway. With one last glance around the converted porch room, Rachel ran through the house and out the front door.

Anxiously, she watched her father help Grandma out of the back seat. Her mother stood close by with Grandma's overnight case in her hand.

Grandma's legs wobbled, and she gripped Dan Lincoln's arm. Rachel was relieved to see her smile as she took her first uncertain steps up the sidewalk.

"Hi, Grandma! Welcome home!" Rachel jumped down the steps. "You look great!" Mentally she crossed her fingers, sure that God wouldn't mind one little lie.

"Rachel." Her grandmother reached out to her, while keeping a tight hold on Dan Lincoln's arm. She kissed Rachel's cheek softly. "It's wonderful to see you without a window between us."

"I know." Rachel stood awkwardly, suddenly afraid she would say or do the wrong thing. Just then a brown station wagon pulled into the driveway, with Marcia Carlson at the wheel.

"I forgot she was coming today," Rachel said, giving a small wave.

Her grandmother's tired face softened. "She's a kind young woman. She was the only one who asked me if I wanted to spend my last weeks at home."

Rachel sucked in her breath sharply. Before she could reply, Beverly Lincoln broke in smoothly. "Don't say that, Mother. In a few weeks you'll feel like your old self and go back to your own house. So, no more talk like that."

Rachel noticed the lonely expression that crossed Grandma's face. Puzzled, Rachel turned at the sound of a car door slamming.

"Hello!" her dad called out. "I see you had no trouble following us. Come in."

Nurse Carlson nodded cheerfully, examining the house as she strolled up the walk. "It's nice coming here during the daytime. You have a lovely yard."

"You should see the backyard," Rachel said. "Most of the flowers are out there. We turned our enclosed porch into Grandma's bedroom, and she can smell the peonies through the window by her bed."

"That sounds lovely and restful." Nurse Carlson glanced at Grandma, whose face looked pinched. "Speaking of rest, Mrs. Potter, I think we'd better check out that new bedroom of yours. Coming home can be very tiring–and certainly enough excitement for one day."

"I don't think I'll argue today," Grandma said with small gasps between her words. Deep lines had formed around her mouth while in the hospital, and her skin seemed stretched too tightly over her hollow cheeks.

Rachel held the screen door as her father and mother led Grandma inside and through the house to the back porch. She would be glad when Grandma got settled in. Then maybe they could talk together, just the two of them.

"Nurse Carlson?" Rachel hung back from the others. "Is there anything I shouldn't talk about with Grandma? I don't want to make her upset."

"First of all, please call me Marcia." The nurse's smile revealed two large front teeth, one slightly overlapping the other. "I understand your fear of upsetting her. She has had a rough two weeks. But I suggest you treat her normally—that will help her recovery tremendously."

Rachel dug the toe of her tennis shoe into the carpet, wondering how to ask her next question. "Grandma looks thin and weak, but I expected that."

"But?" Marcia prompted.

"But she also looks so sad . . . kind of hopeless."

Marcia motioned for Rachel to sit down on the carpeted stairs. The nurse joined Rachel, her long legs stretched out and crossed at the ankle.

"Your grandmother is trying to recover from two very hard blows. One is the surgery she had two weeks ago. In another month or so she should be fully recovered from that." The nurse paused, then took one of Rachel's hands in her own. "The other blow is much harder to handle, but Mrs. Potter is making much progress."

"What other blow?" Rachel asked quietly, grateful that at last someone was willing to answer her questions.

"Every single human being has to face his or her death at some time. We all avoid the issue, although we'll have to face it sooner or later. It's always a blow when we realize we have less time left than we'd thought." Marcia Carlson lowered her voice slightly. "Your grandmother, and you and your family too, are trying to adjust to this knowledge. It's life's hardest adjustment, and it takes time."

"But couldn't the cancer just disappear? Like in a miracle?" Rachel rushed on. "My brother Brent says it can happen that way."

"It can," Marcia said carefully. "I've seen cases where the doctors gave up hope, but the patient lived for years after that."

Rachel's heart grew fifty pounds lighter. "Really? You know, I thought Mom and Dad were trying to keep something from me. I guess I misunderstood—"

"But," Marcia interrupted softly, "I don't know if Mrs. Potter fits into that category or not. A lot will depend on your grandmother's state of mind, so being cheerful whenever possible is helpful."

"That's what Mom and Dad told me."

"On the other hand, don't hide your true feelings from her. She'll sense it and be hurt by it. I'm convinced we should use this time to sit, listen, and share our feelings."

Rachel took a deep breath. "I've always shared things with Grandma. That shouldn't be hard."

"Let's go see how your grandmother is doing." Marcia Carlson stood up, pulling Rachel with her. "Any time you have a question, call me. I've left my number with your mother. I promise to be as honest with you as I can."

Rachel studied the young nurse, sensing again that she was a friend who could be counted on. Together they walked down the hall to Grandma's new room.

Grandma sat in bed, propped up by two pillows. Marcia perched on the edge of the bed. "How are you feeling, Mrs. Potter?"

"Tired mostly. And please call me Minna. So few people do anymore. When you grow old, there is no one left to call you by your first name."

"I'd love to, Minna." Marcia patted Grandma's arm gently. "I understand what you mean. After being called Nurse Carlson all day, I almost forget I have a first name."

After Marcia Carlson visited with Grandma for several minutes, she stood to leave. Rachel's parents walked out with her. Rachel could hear her parents' hushed voices as they talked to the nurse near the front door.

Grandma frowned slightly. "I wish people wouldn't do that."

"Do what?" Rachel pulled up the small rocking chair near the bed.

"Whisper about me just out of earshot. As if I didn't know what they were talking about." She picked at the lace on her bed jacket. "This is a pretty room you've all fixed up for me. I can't imagine a lovelier place to spend my last weeks."

The hairs on Rachel's neck prickled and she shivered. "Mom says you shouldn't talk that way. Nurse Carlson said she'd had patients live years longer than the doctors had predicted. You're going to be one of them, Grandma."

Grandma Potter reached out and touched Rachel's hand. "Maybe. But I feel so very tired, Rachel. I think God is preparing me to go home to be with Him."

"No! That's not true!" Rachel lowered her voice. "Before long you'll be as good as new. You'll be home in no time."

"We'll see." Grandma closed her eyes wearily. "Will you do me a favor, just in case I don't go back home to live?"

"Sure, Grandma. What?"

"Your mother doesn't have room here for all my plants and potted flowers. Could you give them away?"

"I don't think that's a good idea." Rachel shook her head decidedly. "I'll water them for you every week, but I won't give them away. When you move back home, you'll miss all your beautiful plants."

Her grandmother opened her eyes and stared sadly at Rachel, as if searching for some answer in her face. Rachel grew uncomfortable and moved the rocker back into the corner.

"I guess I'd better let you sleep. The nurse said you would need a lot of rest these first couple of weeks."

When she leaned over to kiss her grandmother's cheek, Grandma Potter whispered in her ear. "Thank you for thinking of my books and your grandfather's picture. It *was* you who brought them here, wasn't it?"

Rachel nodded, pleased that she had done something right. "If you think of anything else you want, just tell me." Rachel tiptoed out of Grandma's new bedroom.

In the next weeks, Rachel watched her grandmother closely. She slept a great deal at first, waking only long enough to sip some broth or read a while. Rachel visited her cheerful porch room often, but tried not to stay too long.

Marcia Carlson visited twice the first week, then began her regular Wednesday checkups. Rachel looked forward to these days and hurried home after school in order not to miss her.

The young nurse gradually adjusted Grandma's menus to include soft foods like mashed potatoes and chopped meat. Grandma's appetite picked up, and she seemed to enjoy her food more.

The first giant milestone occurred three weeks after she came home. Grandma joined Rachel's family at the kitchen table for supper. It was a red letter day for the whole family.

Grandma's spirits improved almost as much as her physical health. The sad, longing look slowly disappeared from her eyes, and she stopped talking about dying. One day she even mentioned to Rachel that she needed to hire a neighbor boy to mow her lawn and weed her flowers. She didn't want her yard to look neglected when she moved back home.

Several days later Rachel hurried home from school and into Grandma's room as usual. When she saw that she was dozing, she started to back out.

"Don't go, Rachel, I'm awake. Just resting my eyes." Grandma straightened her pink quilted robe. "I've been wondering what's happened to your young friends. You used to bring Kara and Jim to my house a lot. Do you see them anymore?"

"Just at school mostly. They're both busy, and I've been—" She stopped abruptly.

"—coming straight home every day after school to keep me company," Grandma finished for her with a knowing smile. "I realize you've given up time with your friends to spend it with me."

"I don't mind, honestly." Rachel tucked one foot underneath her in the rocking chair. "I like talking to you."

"But you need your friends too. That's why I've been thinking."

"About what?"

"That it's time you learned to do some needlework. Maybe a cross-stitch sampler, to begin with. I'd be happy to teach Kara how to sew at the same time," Grandma offered. "What do you think about that?"

Rachel leaned forward excitedly. "I think that's a great idea! I'm sure Kara would love it too. When can we start?"

"Tomorrow. Stop by my house on the way home from school and bring me my sewing basket—the big blue one. It has all the material and embroidery floss we'll need. You girls can choose your patterns tomorrow."

Rachel jumped up, and the rocker hit the wall behind her. "I'm going to go call Kara. I can't wait until tomorrow to get started."

"Just a minute. I have a secret to tell you." Grandma Potter peered over Rachel's shoulder at the empty door, then whispered, "I haven't told anyone else, but you and I understand each other. I want you to know that I've been cured."

Rachel felt her mouth fall open, and she deliberately closed it. "Cured? You really think so?"

"Yes, I do." Grandma gripped Rachel's arm. "I prayed and prayed for God to heal me. I promised Him I wouldn't spend any more of my life on selfish things. And He's answered me. I'm cured!"

Rachel didn't know what to say. With all her heart, she wanted to believe it. She had to admit that Grandma certainly looked and acted better.

Rachel chose her words carefully. "Nothing would make me happier, Grandma. If you are cured, pretty soon everyone else will see it for themselves."

With a lighter heart than she'd had in weeks, Rachel went to phone Kara. Maybe her grandmother really *was* cured! She *was* one of the rare lucky ones! Ignoring the doubts in the back of her mind, Rachel was glad to pretend life was getting back to normal.

The next afternoon Rachel chose an old-fashioned sampler to sew. It had rows of numbers and the alphabet around the edges, and "Home Sweet Home" in the center, surrounded by violets.

Day by day, with each additional small cross, she watched the picture take shape. Kara's pattern was in shades of pink and red, showing a cupid with two intertwined hearts. Rachel shuddered elaborately, but Kara said it was terribly romantic.

For the next two weeks Kara tagged along home from school with Rachel every afternoon. They sewed on their embroidery while telling Grandma about their day at school, exaggerating their humdrum classes and teachers in order to make Grandma laugh.

One Wednesday afternoon Kara bent her braces and had to see her orthodontist. So Rachel came home alone. When she spotted Marcia's car in the driveway, she hurried up the steps. The previous week Marcia had confided she'd become engaged, and she was anxious to ask her more about it.

But thoughts of Marcia's engagement flew from her mind when Rachel reached the porch doorway. Marcia leaned over the bed, laying a wet washcloth on Grandma's forehead. Rachel's grandmother was deathly white; her shallow breathing barely moved the blanket.

Marcia glanced up, putting a finger to her lips. Rachel backed out of the room. Marcia waited a moment, but when Grandma didn't stir, the nurse joined Rachel in the hall.

"Let's go into the kitchen," she whispered. Rachel nodded and followed the nurse down the hall. Her mother was already seated at the kitchen table, holding a coffee cup and eating corn chips.

Rachel shifted from one foot to the other. "What's the matter with Grandma?"

Her mother's cup clinked loudly in the saucer. "This was Grandma's day for chemotherapy at the hospital. She got a stronger dose and her body's reacting more severely this time." Although she spoke matter-of-factly, the lines around her mouth deepened.

Rachel knew Grandma had been going to the hospital once a week for a blood test and her chemotherapy. She had even gone once herself—it only took an hour. On the days of the treatments, Grandma couldn't eat because of the nausea it brought on. Dr. Osborne said it was a necessary precaution to keep the cancer from spreading.

Pouring herself a cup of coffee, Marcia brought it to the table. "Are you hungry?" she asked Rachel.

"No." Rachel collapsed onto a kitchen chair. "Is there something no one's telling me?"

Rachel caught the questioning glance that passed between Marcia and her mother. After a short pause her mother nodded at the nurse.

Marcia reached for a peanut butter cookie from the panda-shaped jar on the table. "As your mom said, Minna is having a harder time today with the chemotherapy. She's nauseated and just plain aches all over."

She broke the cookie in tiny pieces. "But you're right. Today was different."

"Did something happen at the hospital?"

"Dr. Osborne came and talked with us before her chemotherapy. He'd run some tests last week and wanted to share the results with us." Marcia paused, reducing her cookie to a pile of crumbs. "I'm afraid the test results are not what we'd hoped for."

Rachel fought the panic that threatened to choke her. Suddenly angry, she didn't want to believe Marcia. "Mom?"

Rachel's mother crumpled the empty chip bag. "I'm afraid Dr. Osborne's tests showed the cancer is growing again." She squeezed Rachel's fingers until the knuckles turned white.

"But Grandma's been so much better lately! She's talking about moving home soon! And you *know* she's much stronger than when she first came home. She *can't* be getting worse!" Rachel stood up suddenly. Her chair fell over backwards with a crash.

"Rachel, wait!" Her mom grabbed her arm, but Rachel roughly shook off her hand. As she stumbled from the room, Rachel heard Marcia's words.

"Let her go for now."

Taking the stairs two at a time, Rachel ran until she was in her own room with the door locked. Collapsing on the floor, she rested her head on the windowsill.

It just couldn't be true! Dr. Osborne's tests must

be wrong. Obviously he'd mixed up Grandma's test results with someone else's. Rachel knew that if the cancer had started growing again, she would have known!

Ten minutes later, Rachel left the window, her anger spent. Without wanting to, she recalled Marcia's words the day Grandma had come home from the hospital. She'd been trying to prepare her, even then, for the possibility that Grandma wouldn't live very long.

Remembering, Rachel rummaged in her top dresser drawer, under some lacy slips. There, wrapped in her old Easter dress, were five clothespin dolls in yellow dotted Swiss. Rachel lined them up on her dresser in a neat row. Somewhere, deep inside her, Rachel knew that Dr. Osborne's test results were right.

But it just wasn't fair! Grandma was a *good* person. She did so many kind things for other people. She bet her grandmother never had an enemy in her whole life. It wasn't right, and it wasn't fair.

By the next day after school, most of the side effects of the chemotherapy had worn off. Grandma sat up in bed, holding a piece of needlework. Rachel's grandmother was rarely awake without holding something to sew or read.

"Hi, Grandma." Rachel leaned over and kissed her cheek. "What are you sewing today?"

"I'm starting a basket of flowers. Today I got two

pansies and a snapdragon done. How do you like the colors?" Grandma held out the round sewing frame for Rachel's inspection.

"They're pretty. You must be feeling a lot better to have finished so much today." Rachel curled up in her favorite rocker.

"Yes, I am better. After what Dr. Osborne said yesterday, I decided to start one more sewing project. I hope I can get it finished." Her smile faded. "I may not have this much strength for long."

"Don't say that, Grandma. Please."

"But I'm afraid it's something we both have to face, honey." She sewed three more purple stitches on a pansy. "I know it's hard, but we'll make it."

"But it isn't *fair*, Grandma! I need you! You can't leave me!"

"I know it isn't fair. I know it. I hate being a financial and emotional drain on people. I'm even jealous of my friends who still have their health." She turned toward the window. "But I must believe God knows what He's doing."

"How can you say that? If this is how God takes care of you, I don't think I like your God very much! It's senseless!"

Grandma handed her sewing hoop to Rachel. "Look at the underside of the sewing, at the back side of the hoop."

Rachel turned the hoop over, then glanced up curiously.

"See all these tangled threads? Someone once told me that those tangled knots of light and dark threads are like man's view of his life. It's a mixture of good and bad times, but it doesn't make any sense when you look at it."

"That's *exactly* how I feel."

"Turn the hoop over now to the flower design. This is like God's view of our lives. Although it looks like a tangled mess to *us*, He knows the real reason for each light and dark thread. This difficult time right now is one of those dark threads."

Rachel traced the outlines of both pansies. "Do you *really* think God has a reason for your sickness? I just can't believe that." Her voice sounded as hard as the rock on her necklace.

"It's all right to be angry, Rachel. Sometimes I still am too. But after a while, somehow we'll both have to learn to accept it."

Rachel jumped up, the sewing hoop falling to the floor with a clatter. "Well, I *won't* accept it, Grandma! I can't!" Without a backward glance, Rachel turned and stumbled from her grandmother's room.

5

Old Friends

RACHEL KEPT Marcia's words locked inside herself all week. Twice she started to tell Kara about it, but the phrase "Grandma's dying" stuck in her throat. Rachel feared if she actually voiced those words, it would come true. So instead she took Kara home each day after school, never admitting a thing.

She and Kara sewed under Grandma's instruction for nearly an hour every day. After two weeks their samplers were nearly completed. If Kara noticed the changes in Grandma, she kept them to herself.

With the addition of each tiny cross-stitch,

Rachel secretly studied her grandmother. More and more often Grandma had to stop sewing and lie back against her down-filled pillows. As the days passed, she listened more and talked less.

One Saturday morning Rachel grabbed a grimy pair of gardening gloves and headed for the backyard to weed her mother's rose beds. When she was troubled about something, the best place to concentrate was down on her knees in the dirt.

Rachel liked to work in the rose garden. It was a peaceful place to think, alone. She worked methodically, carefully avoiding the thorns. Her worries were interrupted by a familiar piercing whistle coming from the corner of the house.

Jim! She hadn't heard his shrill whistle on Saturday morning for a long time.

Brushing the dirt from her knees, Rachel walked toward her black-haired friend. "Howdy, stranger. Where'd you drift in from?" She stood with feet planted wide and spoke in her best Western drawl.

"Just roundin' up my posse, Ma'am." Jim hooked his thumbs in his belt loops. "Indians on the war path again."

Rachel laughed at the familiar lines, and it felt good. Jim's grandfather was a full-blooded Indian; as kids, they had played Indians, using his grandfather's real beaded leather shirts and bows without the arrows.

She peered up at the sky, blue and smooth as a

robin's egg. "It's already hot, for so early. Want to go fishing this afternoon?" Rachel hadn't been to Vandermeer's Pond since the previous fall.

"Sounds great, but I can't this afternoon. Steve and I are working on a new song." Tilting his head to one side, his black hair fell over one eye. "Want to come with me? You could listen to the song and give us your opinion."

Rachel's enthusiasm for the day oozed from her like helium from a leaky balloon. She'd hoped they could go fishing that afternoon, just the two of them.

She pivoted on her heel. "No thanks! I can think of a million better things to do than sit in Steve Forrester's garage all afternoon, getting a headache from you beating your drums." She stalked over to the nearest rose bush and yanked at a stubborn weed.

"I just thought maybe you'd like to come—"

"Forget it!" Rachel threw the weed over her shoulder. It landed on Jim's foot, spraying tiny clods of mud. "Maybe we'll go sometime when you're not so *busy*."

Jim backed up two steps, shaking the mud from his shoe. "I just thought—you know—I haven't seen you much lately."

"Whose fault is that?" Rachel demanded.

Even as she spoke, she hated the spiteful tone of her voice. But she couldn't help it.

She wanted to go fishing, just the two of them.

Words came so easily when she was with Jim. Rachel wanted to confide in him about Grandma dying. Just by listening, he would have helped her.

"Yeah, well . . . I'll see you at school, I guess." Jim shoved his hands deep in the pockets of his Levi's, then turned and slouched around the corner of the house.

Rachel rocked back on her heels. *Nothing* turned out right these days. Grandma and Jim were the two people in the whole world she was closest to But Jim was too busy for her, and Grandma was—slipping away.

Gritting her teeth, Rachel snapped off a nearby daffodil. She demolished it, petal by yellow petal, then tossed the bare stem to the ground. Still angry, she attacked the rest of the weeds.

Without stopping, Rachel drove herself hard for another hour. By the time the last weed lay wilting in the sun, she had worked off much of her anger at Jim.

However, the knot in the pit of her stomach persisted. Had she overreacted when Jim invited her to Steve's house? Probably, but it was too late now to fix it. She wiped her dirty, scratched hands on the grass and headed for the cool house.

Rachel decided to eat lunch with Grandma and carried her tray of food out to the porch. For the past week, Grandma had been too exhausted to join them for meals. Just getting up and dressed tired her, so she had most of her meals in bed.

Rachel munched noisily on her celery smeared with peanut butter. Glancing up, she caught her grandmother's worried look.

"Rachel, you don't seem very happy for such a pretty day. Did you get scratched up out in the rose bushes?"

"You might say that." Rachel licked her gooey fingers. "Jim was here. He wanted me to listen to him and Steve practice a new song this afternoon. I told him I had better things to do."

"I know. I honestly didn't mean to, but I couldn't help overhearing you and Jim. I woke up from my nap in the middle of your conversation. Being so close to these porch windows, your voices carried easily."

"Then you know how he's been treating me." Rachel jerked the rocker forward, irritated all over again. "Saturdays used to be *our* day. Now he's always too busy playing basketball or practicing with that dumb band of his."

Grandma shakily lifted a small spoonful of poached egg to her mouth. "Do you still like Jim? Do you want his friendship, or have you outgrown each other?"

"I still like Jim, Grandma. A lot. He's the easiest person to talk to, next to you. But for some reason, since we changed schools, he's too busy to do anything with me."

"But he invited you to go with him this afternoon, didn't he?"

Rachel jabbed her knee with a stalk of celery. "That's just it, though. We'd have been with Steve too, and who knows how many other people. I can't talk to Jim with an audience."

"In other words, you want to be Jim's friend, but you don't want him to have any other friends?" Grandma asked, wheezing slightly.

"That's not true!"

"Probably not. But I'll bet that's how it sounds to Jim." Grandma picked at the fleecy yellow bedspread.

"But, Grandma—"

"You can't *demand* a friend's attention, Rachel, no matter how much you want to. People won't tolerate that for long."

Rachel flopped back in the rocker, speechless. Was that how it really looked? Her grandmother just didn't understand. She had *had* to demand Jim's attention lately. Otherwise she'd never see him anymore.

Rachel pulled a long string from her celery stalk. "Jim and I used to spend lots of time together. But now, if I didn't remind him sometimes, he'd never come over."

"That may be true." Grandma reached for Rachel's hand. "But you mustn't hang on so tightly to him. If you stop nagging him, and then he stops coming over, you would have drifted apart sooner or later anyway."

Rachel clamped her teeth together until her jaw ached. Grandma didn't understand at all, but in her weak condition, Rachel felt she shouldn't argue with her.

She admitted to herself that Grandma might be right about Jim, and about holding on too tight. But one thing Rachel felt sure of: if you didn't hang on to the people you loved, they slowly slipped away.

6

Time Out

SECRETLY, Rachel was relieved the next week when Kara finished her cupid and hearts cross-stitch project and stopped coming home with her every afternoon.

Kara asked too many pointed questions about Grandma. Why was she so quiet? Why didn't she ever eat anything when they had a snack after school? And even why was her hair falling out?

Rachel made excuses, blaming the medicine for Grandma's sleepiness and lack of appetite. She hated lying to her best friend, but she just couldn't talk about Grandma's sickness yet.

On the days Grandma had chemotherapy, Rachel went straight home after school. She wanted Grandma to know she was there if she needed her.

Rachel also began to notice that her mother was exhausted by the constant nursing care. The strain showed in her glassy stare and the new lines around her eyes and mouth.

It wasn't that Grandma was a bad patient. She really complained little. Rachel guessed it had more to do with being cooped up in the too-quiet house. She'd heard her mother's wistful voice when talking on the phone once. It sounded like she missed her friends from the Garden Club and Tuesday Music Club she'd always attended.

Rachel guessed her mom's days were awfully long and boring. She'd given up her nine piano students weeks before, recommending other teachers. She was afraid the noise would bother Grandma. She spent her whole week nursing Grandma.

The following Wednesday afternoon Rachel eased open the front door and slipped into the house. Stacking her school books at the bottom of the carpeted staircase, she tiptoed down the hall to the porch bedroom.

Statue-like, her mother sat motionless in the rocker. Her hands were folded limply in her lap while she stared out the window. Grandma appeared to be sleeping.

"Mom?" Rachel whispered softly. "How did Grandma's chemotherapy treatment go today?"

Rachel's mother blinked twice, as if coming out of a trance, then rose quietly from the rocking chair. "About the same as last week. I sure hope this chemotherapy is helping, because it makes her awfully sick."

"Did you talk to Dr. Osborne?"

"Yes. He wants her to keep coming for the treatments. He can't tell yet if it's doing any good." Rachel's mother rubbed her eyes tiredly. "Your grandmother seems to handle things all right, but her sickness is starting to get *me* down."

Rachel watched the still form in the bed. The blanket barely moved with Grandma's breathing. "I'll sit with her for a while, in case she wakes up."

Rachel's mother ran fingers through her tousled hair. "Thanks, honey. I do need to get supper started. Maybe I'll go outside for a minute first. I'll bring in a flower for Grandma's table."

Rachel curled up in her mother's place in the rocker. The bright porch, silent except for Grandma's shallow breathing, usually had a calming effect on her. The room had grown comfortably familiar—from the lemon-yellow gingham curtains and her grandfather's picture to the wicker basket of unfinished sewing by the bed.

A soft moan snapped Rachel to attention.

Hovering over the bed, she examined her grandmother's ashen face. Her translucent eyelids fluttered occasionally as she breathed through slightly parted dry lips.

Rachel gently touched her grandmother's forehead. The dry skin seemed hot to her. Slipping down the hall to the bathroom, Rachel wrung out a wash cloth in cold water. Back on the porch, she folded it and laid it on Grandma's forehead.

As she stood there, Rachel detected a slight rustling noise under the window. She moved around the bed and peered through the screen.

After clipping off last year's dead rose blooms, her mother carefully cut three yellow and orange daffodils. Holding the flowers close, she breathed deeply, then glanced up at the window and smiled at Rachel.

Rachel waved, then went to rinse the wash cloth again. It had turned hot quickly. Back on the porch, she laid it softly on Grandma's forehead. She hoped it somehow made Grandma feel better.

If only she could think of something more important to do. Sometimes she felt so useless.

She studied the changes in her grandmother's face. There were dark circles around her eyes these days, almost bluish-purple. Her skin looked like white tissue paper tautly stretched. As Rachel stood quietly, she saw tears appear under the edges of Grandma's eyelashes. They slowly collected at the outside corners of her closed eyes. Grandma still appeared asleep, but the tears welled up and slipped over the sides of her face. They flowed down the zigzag creases in her cheeks, like following a crooked river on a map.

Rachel gently picked up Grandma's hand. The blue veins on the back of her hand were prominent; large brown spots were scattered there and up her arms. Grandma called them "old lady's hands," but to Rachel they were beautiful.

Then, standing by the bed watching Grandma sleep, Rachel finally faced the fact that her grandmother was really dying. She'd tried her best not to see the signs—the increased weakness, the loss of appetite. But other signs were harder to ignore.

Each week her reaction to the chemotherapy was worse. The aching and nausea lasted longer; sores had developed in her mouth that made it hard to eat.

And her hair *was* falling out. Rachel had removed clumps of loose hair from the pillow when Grandma wasn't looking, then brushed her gray curls into fluffiness to disguise how thin it was becoming.

Rachel wished for the thousandth time that she could really help Grandma. She'd do anything, give up anything, just to see her get well.

She turned at the sound of footsteps. Her mom carried a cut glass vase, holding three peachy-orange daffodils. "How do you like these?" Her mother placed the vase on the night table. "They're lasting real well this spring."

"Grandma will love to see them when she wakes up."

"Has she stirred yet?"

Rachel hesitated, remembering the silent tears trickling down Grandma's cheeks. "No, she hasn't opened her eyes at all."

Rachel changed into some cut-offs and a tank top, grabbed a spy novel, and went outside to read. Leaning against the trunk of a stately old shagbark hickory, she tried to concentrate on who had kidnapped the book's young heroine.

But she couldn't get involved in the suspense story. Finally she closed the book, slid down flat on her back, and gazed up through the scraggly black branches.

When had the jade-green of summer replaced the chartreuse of spring in the clusters of leaves overhead? Spring was nearly gone, but Rachel felt she had missed it that year. It had arrived without her noticing.

She was saddened that life was going on, just as it always had, but amazed too. How could everything be the same, when her own private world had come to a dead stop?

Rachel lay under the tree thinking, until dusk, but she found no answers. That night she slept fitfully. At four o'clock in the morning she jerked upright in her bed, gasping.

The image from her dream was so vivid! She'd just dreamed that Grandma had called to her, wanting to say good-bye. Her heart pounding, Rachel had tried to hurry down the stairs to Grandma's bedroom. But her legs were leaden and moved in slow motion, as if she were running through deep water.

When she got to the porch, Grandma was gone! Instead, the room was just as before, full of wicker summer furniture, tennis rackets, and trays of flower seedlings.

Rachel shivered as cold sweat ran down her sides under her cotton pajamas. She knew it was just a dream, but the picture of Grandma saying good-bye was so real! She lay back on her pillow, staring up into the dark.

The harder Rachel tried to fall asleep, the more wide awake she grew. She felt as if she were suffocating—she was weighed down by the sense that something was terribly wrong.

What if her dream was a warning? What if Grandma was dying right at that very minute? Maybe she needed something, but was too weak to call for help!

Rachel sat up in bed and hugged her knees. She knew she'd never sleep until she checked on Grandma. Throwing off the limp sheet, she tiptoed to her bedroom door and listened hard. There was no sound, so she moved out into the hall.

Her fingertips brushed the rough plastered wall as she inched her way down the hall. The thudding of her heart was so loud in her ears that she was sure someone would hear it.

When Rachel reached the top of the landing, it

was lighter. Moving swiftly, she glided down the carpeted steps and through the front entry. Turning, she headed down the short hall to the back porch. There Rachel stopped, peering into the faint gray light that filtered through the porch screens.

Rachel held her breath, listening.

There was no sound but a soft breeze whispering in the elms outside the window. She crept closer to the bed. When her outstretched fingers touched the bedspread, she stopped again and leaned closer.

As her eyes adjusted to the shadows, she could almost distinguish the small hump in the covers that was Grandma's sleeping form. She lay so still! Rachel bent close to her face and held her breath again.

The unbroken silence stretched on forever. Finally Rachel heard a faint, yet unmistakable, slight wheezing sound. Grandma was breathing! Rachel almost cried with relief.

Her dream had been a lie. Grandma was fine, Rachel told herself.

And yet, she hated to go back upstairs. Just in case . . . So she tiptoed to the rocking chair, picked up the afghan folded on the seat, and eased herself down onto the padded cushion.

When the chair's joints creaked, she froze. But Grandma didn't stir, so Rachel carefully unfolded the afghan and wrapped it around her legs.

Curled up in the corner of the chair, she finally relaxed, knowing she was nearby in case Grandma needed anything during the rest of the night. She closed her eyes wearily.

Sunlight streaming through the porch windows woke Rachel the next morning. She groaned and massaged her knotted neck muscles. Her grandmother lay in bed, watching her.

Rachel struggled to an upright position. "Hi, Grandma. Been awake long?" she asked sheepishly.

"Long enough to wonder why you're sleeping in my chair." She frowned slightly. "Are you all right, honey?"

"Sure, Grandma." Rachel busied herself folding the afghan. "I couldn't sleep last night. I came down to see if you were awake and wanted to talk or anything."

"That's odd. I've never known you to have insomnia. Remember when you stayed overnight with me last summer? You slept right through that tornado that ripped through town."

Rachel sighed. Sometimes Grandma knew her too well. "I had a scary dream last night," she finally admitted. "I was afraid something was wrong. When I sneaked downstairs, though, you were sleeping fine. So I curled up in the chair in case you woke up."

"Come here, Rachel." Grandma stretched a thin arm towards her.

Rachel leaned against the bed. "It was a horrible nightmare. I dreamed you died."

"I know this is frightening for you." Grandma

squeezed Rachel's hand. "Just remember, there's nothing we can't talk about. Including dying."

"Aren't you afraid to die, Grandma?"

"No, not anymore. Really sad, but not afraid." Grandma stared out the window for a moment. "For me, dying isn't the end. It's really a new beginning."

"I don't understand."

Grandma turned back to her, tilting her head to one side. "It's kind of like when you were born."

"How? That doesn't make sense."

"When Beverly was expecting you, she was so excited. She could hardly wait for you to be born. However, you might have preferred to stay within your mother, where it was warm and safe."

Rachel smiled at that idea. "Nobody asked me though!"

"That's right. It wasn't your choice. You were born into this world to begin your new life."

Rachel frowned. "But dying is the opposite of being born."

"Not really. When you were born, you just changed the place you lived—from living *inside* your mother to living *outside*. For me, dying is the same thing."

"I still don't get it."

"Dying just means I won't be living here with you anymore. To me, heaven is a real place, but I won't pretend I'm anxious, or even ready, to go there right now." Grandma gave Rachel a wry smile. "But, like you, I didn't have any 'say so' when I was born. It won't be my choice when I die."

"I'm not ready either. I won't *ever* be ready." Her chest tightened at the sadness in Grandma's eyes. "I'll go get us some breakfast." Rachel didn't think she could swallow a bite, but she knew her grandmother needed to eat.

"No thanks, Rachel, I don't care for any." Grandma waved her hand listlessly toward the window. "You know, I'll never see another spring."

Rachel shifted from one foot to the other. She didn't know how to answer, so she ignored her grandmother's words.

"You need to eat *something*. I'll fix whatever you'd like. Then I'll come back and eat with you."

Grandma lay back and closed her eyes. "I'd rather be left alone, Rachel. I'm not good company. I hope you can understand."

"Um, sure."

Rachel backed out of the room, partly relieved to go, but also kind of hurt that Grandma didn't want her company. She padded down the hall toward the voices in the kitchen, but paused in the doorway at the harsh anger in her father's words.

"But why can't we accept Mark and Susan's invitation? We haven't been out of the house together for months!"

"You know I can't leave Mother!" Beverly's voice was shrill and tight.

"Brent and Rachel could sit with your mother. We'd leave the doctor's and restaurant's phone numbers in case of an emergency." The coaxing note in her dad's voice barely concealed the anger.

"No, I just can't. How would that look? My mother here, *dying of cancer*, and you and I going out?" Her mother sounded close to tears.

"Look, Beverly! I'm suffocating in this house! You are too. You never get out, even to the grocery store. Brent and I have bought all the groceries for weeks. You need a change of scenery, even just for an hour or two. Please, let's accept Mark and Susan's invitation."

"I can't!"

"All right!" Her father stomped toward the back door. "But when I get home from work tonight, *I'm* changing and going out for dinner. I need to get out of here sometimes." The back door slammed as Rachel's father left for work.

Rachel backed down the hall quietly. Suddenly she didn't want to see or talk to anybody.

Grandma wanted to be left alone, her father felt suffocated in the house, and her mother was probably crying in the kitchen. Although she felt overwhelming guilt, Rachel suddenly wanted to leave the house as desperately as her dad did.

Upstairs, she grabbed the hall phone from its small round table. Unwinding the extra long cord as she went, she carried the phone into her bedroom and dialed Kara's number.

"Kara? Let's go to a movie this afternoon!" Rachel was determined to sound cheerful, even if she had to fake it.

"What's playing?"

"I don't know. At this point I'll watch anything." Rachel didn't care what movie played on the screen, as long as it made her forget everything at home for a couple hours.

"Let me get the newspaper." Kara was gone for a minute, then back. The crackle of rustling paper came over the phone. "You're in luck. They're having a cartoon revue at the Strand–you love those. Says there'll be clips from over twenty classics. How about that?"

"Perfect." Rachel had a passion for old cartoons. The theater would be jammed with screaming little kids, guaranteed to keep her from thinking. "I'll pick you up at one. The treat's on me, Kara. I know you don't really like these cartoon revues."

"No, that's okay. But the next time we see a romantic love story, okay?"

Rachel grinned into the phone. "It's a deal. See you in a couple of hours."

Rachel spent the rest of the morning in her room,

clearing the clutter from her desk, then doing her homework. Her mother knocked on her door once, but left her alone after that. Rachel was glad, but it made her feel even more like a deserter.

By one-thirty, she and Kara were slouched in lumpy front row seats at the shabby old Strand Theater, munching buttered popcorn. Although Rachel hadn't had any appetite for breakfast or lunch, suddenly she was ravenous.

While waiting for the lights to dim, Rachel unwillingly remembered her morning. She pictured Grandma in bed at home, staring sadly out the window at her last spring.

And how was *she* spending her afternoon? Laughing at old cartoons and stuffing her face! How insensitive could she be?

Her depression of the morning settled over her like a heavy wool blanket.

The theater soon overflowed with shrieking children of all ages. Rachel was grateful for all the confusion. Even if she'd wanted to think, it would have been impossible. She settled back, prepared to lose herself in ninety minutes of old Mickey Mouse, Donald Duck, and Yogi Bear cartoons.

An hour and a half later, Rachel had finished her popcorn, two coconut candy bars, and a box of Jujubes. Sighing, she collected her empty wrappers and boxes. Her face ached from laughing, as if she'd used facial muscles that hadn't been exercised in months.

Rachel knew she'd really needed that breather. She'd enjoyed her "time out" even more than she'd expected. Linking her arm through Kara's, they left the theater.

It was time to return to the real world.

7

Gladys

WHEN RACHEL arrived home from the cartoon revue, the door to Grandma's room was closed, so she went to the kitchen. Her mother sat at the table, munching corn chips and leaning on one elbow as she leafed through her Betty Crocker cookbook.

"How was the revue?" she asked, closing the book.

"Great. It felt good to laugh again." Rachel studied her mother's despondent expression. "Maybe you *should* go out with Dad tonight. It might help you feel better."

"You heard us this morning?"

"I wasn't listening, honest. I was in the hall, and your voices were kind of loud." She paused, remembering the closed porch door. "Is Grandma asleep?"

"No, but she doesn't want to talk to anyone this afternoon." Rachel's mother reached deep into the chip bag. "Do you remember her neighbor, Mrs. Butler? She came by after you left for the movie, but Grandma wouldn't even see her."

"That's not like Grandma," Rachel said, surprised. "She's never rude to her friends."

"I don't think she's being rude. She's depressed, but I can't seem to help." Rachel's mother picked at the fingernail polish on her thumbnail. "I tried to talk to her about it, but she asked me to leave her alone. So I did."

Rachel stood awkwardly, not knowing what to say. She had felt "shut out" by Grandma lately too. She wished she could talk to Marcia soon. Rachel knew the young nurse could help them understand.

That night Rachel worked in her room, polishing some of the limestone and slate she'd collected the previous fall. She enjoyed the clatter of the hand-cranked rock polishing machine she'd received last year for Christmas.

Then she took some previously polished agates and quartz and fashioned them into a heart-shaped pin. When she needed some quiet time to herself, she liked to make jewelry and barrettes by hand for Kara and herself.

She hoped her mother was enjoying her book downstairs. Rachel had left her curled up on the couch. She had refused again to leave Grandma, so Rachel's father and Brent left without her. They drove to nearby Junction Falls for a preseason college baseball game.

It was an unusually quiet evening, but not peaceful, Rachel thought. Grandma wouldn't eat any supper and still wanted to be alone. The phone didn't ring once, and nothing on TV seemed appealing. She went to bed at eleven and fell instantly and deeply asleep.

The next afternoon Rachel was relieved to see the porch door open. Grandma sat hunched over, trying to stitch another pansy on her basket design. But as Rachel watched, Grandma threw down the sewing hoop in disgust.

"Having some trouble?" Rachel blinked at Grandma's angry expression. "I can help if your thread is knotted or something."

"There's nothing you can do. I'm just so tired I can hardly see straight." Grandma stuffed her embroidery floss into the basket on her bed. "What are you up to this morning?" She smiled, but Rachel thought it looked forced.

"I came to keep you company." Rachel picked up the silver-handled brush from the night table. "I could brush your hair for you."

"Thank you, Rachel. I know I look frightful these days."

"You don't look frightful, Grandma! Nobody looks their best when they've been sick." Rachel brushed her gray curls gently, but was dismayed to see how much hair came loose in the brush. Grandma's hair got thinner every week.

"That feels good. Is more hair falling out?"

"What do you mean?" Rachel hoped Grandma hadn't noticed.

"I see the hair on my pillow every morning. Sometimes big clumps of it. It won't be long before I'm bald as an egg." Grandma laughed, but her smile never reached her eyes.

"Well, there *is* a bit of hair in the brush, but very little," Rachel fibbed.

"Really?" Grandma turned to her eagerly. "Just between you and me, I hate being a skinny old bag of bones. I don't want to be bald too."

Rachel paused with the brush in midstroke. "Is that why you refused to talk to Mrs. Butler yesterday? You didn't want her to see how you looked?"

Grandma patted her thin hair. "I don't look in mirrors much, but when I do, I see terrible changes. I'm so thin and gaunt now that I'll scare people. I'd rather be remembered how I was a few months ago."

Rachel used her fingers to fluff the hair, trying

to make it look thicker. That technique had worked for several weeks, but Rachel knew it didn't help much now. You could see straight through Grandma's hair to smooth, pink scalp.

"Would you like to have visitors if you wore a hat? It would hide how your hair is thinning." Rachel thought of the pink crocheted cap she'd seen Grandma wear shopping before her illness.

Grandma folded her gnarled hands in her lap. "I don't think a hat would fool anyone. Except for Pastor Rollins, I don't want to see anyone outside the family."

At least Grandma still allowed her minister to come. Except for him, she had cut herself off from the outside world. She no longer saw her friends from the old neighborhood, the ladies from her volunteer team at the hospital, or anyone else outside the immediate family.

Grandma was pulling back, slowly and surely, from the people she cared about.

Rachel softly fluffed Grandma's hair, wishing she felt better about her appearance. Rachel believed Grandma needed friends now more than ever.

When Kara called after lunch, Rachel realized how grateful she was for her own friends. Kara wanted to buy several new teen romances at the book store. Rachel agreed to meet her at the new mall; she arrived as Kara stepped off the bus.

After carefully selecting five paperbacks, Kara

clutched them to her, content then to stroll up and down the airy new mall. Rachel was in no hurry to leave and breathed deeply of the exotic flowers blooming in octagonal-shaped cement planters.

Skylights provided direct sunlight for the waxy orchids and lilies. Rachel wished Grandma could see them. She'd love to sit on a cedar bench and stroke the shiny, perfectly-shaped petals.

Passing the Kut-Rite Beauty Salon, a curly-haired blonde caught Rachel's eye. However, when she turned toward the woman, Rachel laughed aloud. The beautiful "blonde" turned out to be a curly wig on a white, head shaped styrofoam form.

Above the form, a splashy sign announced the Kut-Rite's "going out of business" sale.

Rachel had strolled two stores past the shop when a brilliant idea struck her. She pivoted on her heel without warning.

"Come on, Kara!" She retraced her steps and marched into the beauty shop.

"Wait! What are you doing?"

In less than fifteen minutes, Rachel tried on and bought the blonde curly wig in the shop window. She made a ten-dollar deposit, promising to return the next day with the rest of the money. Hugging the cumbersome round box to her chest, she whistled gaily as they left the mall.

Back home, Rachel smiled mysteriously as she sauntered into the living room. She balanced the round cardboard box on one hand, like a waiter in a fancy restaurant.

Her mother glanced up with a raised eyebrow, but said nothing. Brent was more direct.

"What's in the tub?" He thumped the cardboard box with his knuckle.

"Stop that!" Rachel slid the box onto the coffee table. "Is Grandma awake? I've brought someone to meet her."

Rachel's mother frowned. "Now Rachel, you don't have a pet in there, do you? I can't allow you to take an animal into Grandma's room."

"No animals." Rachel grinned suddenly. "But it's someone Grandma will enjoy meeting. Is she awake?" she asked again.

"I think so."

Rachel carried the round pink cardboard box to the porch and set it on the bed. Grandma closed her book and leaned over. "What's this?"

"Someone for you to meet. Her name's Gladys."

"Gladys?"

"Yes. She's not much in the looks department, but she has a great head of hair." Smiling broadly, Rachel raised the lid and lifted out the head form, complete with curly wig. "This is Gladys."

"What in the world?" Grandma clapped a hand over her mouth.

"I thought about what you said. You know, how

you don't want your friends to see your thinner hair." Rachel played with the blonde curls on the wig. "You can wear Gladys when someone comes to visit."

Grandma's mouth trembled as she laughed silently. "That was very thoughtful of you, honey. But I haven't been a blonde for nearly twenty years!"

"There weren't any gray wigs on sale. Anyway, this is more glamorous." Rachel set it on the dresser across the room. "You don't need it yet, of course. But maybe someday . . ."

Chuckling, Grandma tilted her head to one side. "Gladys's expression *does* leave something to be desired." The white styrofoam head was completely smooth. "How about drawing in a couple of eyes?"

"Sure!" Rachel was pleased with Grandma's acceptance of the gift. Even if she never wore the wig, it had made her smile.

In the bathroom she rummaged through her mother's make-up drawer. Back on the porch, she sketched Gladys a face with eyebrow pencil, used peach blusher to give the white styrofoam cheeks color and contour, and defined her mouth with fire-engine-red lipstick.

Standing back, Rachel surveyed her handiwork. "You're lookin' good, Gladys."

The sound of Grandma's laugh was worth every penny the wig had cost her.

Grandma's spirits were better the next two days.

The porch door remained open, and she encouraged Rachel to visit again. Hope surged through Rachel. Once Grandma told her she believed a last minute breakthrough of some research project would result in a new miracle drug for her.

But after the chemotherapy on Wednesday, Grandma was extremely sick. When Rachel arrived home that afternoon, Marcia Carlson was there.

Rachel wanted to ask Marcia some questions, but the young nurse and her mother were too busy caring for Grandma. Rachel sat slumped at the kitchen table, covering her ears to shut out Grandma's groans and crying. She was sicker than Rachel could ever remember.

The aftereffects lasted three days, and Marcia Carlson and Dr. Osborne visited often. Rachel tried without success to understand their murmured conferences.

Once Rachel watched Marcia give Grandma a pain shot. After that, she ran out when Marcia reached for the needle. But Rachel didn't know which was harder to see—Grandma's pain or her terrible sadness.

On the third afternoon, Marcia emerged from Grandma's room as Rachel entered the house. Rachel glimpsed Marcia's worried expression before the nurse assumed her customary professional smile.

"Is Grandma worse?" Rachel whispered hoarsely.

"No, not at all. She's finally sleeping soundly." Marcia reclipped her loose barrette. "This *was* a strong reaction to the chemotherapy."

"Is that why Grandma's depressed now? Is it from the pain medicine?"

Marcia led Rachel to the living room. "There's more to it than that, although the medication certainly has some effect." She sank gratefully into an overstuffed chair. "But the sadness is very real, Rachel. I'm afraid there's not a lot we can do about it right now."

"Mom says it's real important that we're always cheerful, but I'm not always." Rachel stared down at her hands. "Did I cause Grandma's depression?"

Marcia squeezed Rachel's clenched fists. "You must never think that. I know what your mother means, but right now it wouldn't help Minna to tell her not to be sad."

"Why not?"

"Think how sad you feel losing one person, your grandmother. Minna is adjusting to losing every person and everything she loves. Sometimes the best thing we can do is let her be sad for a while, let her grieve."

Rachel scuffed the toe of her tennis shoe back and forth on the carpet. "Marcia, is Grandma getting any better? Are these chemotherapy treatments helping her at all?"

"You'd have to ask Dr. Osborne about that, I'm afraid."

"But I'm asking *you.*" Rachel stared hard at Marcia.

"Come outside with me. I could use some fresh air and sunshine." Arm in arm, they walked out to sit by the planters overflowing with multicolored impatiens. "I'm not avoiding your question. I honestly don't know if the treatments are helping or not."

"Can Dr. Osborne tell us?"

"He'll have to run some tests first. He plans a series of tests in the next two weeks. Hopefully, he can give you the answer then."

Rachel picked an orange impatien and touched the flower to her cheek. "I doubt that Dr. Osborne will ever tell me what I *really* want to hear—that Grandma is getting well."

Marcia put a slim arm around Rachel's narrow shoulders. They leaned against one another, watching the sun disappear into a sea of frothy pink clouds.

8

Letting Go

THE FOLLOWING Saturday morning when the doorbell rang, Rachel was working on a new bracelet while talking to Grandma. Her mother shouted down the hall.

"Rachel, Jim's here!"

Rachel glanced up in surprise. She was anxious to see Jim, but wondered if he were still angry with her. After she had yelled at him last week, she couldn't blame him.

"I'm coming! Just a minute!" Rachel capped her glue bottle. "Grandma, would you like to see Jim? He asks about you a lot."

"Oh, honey, I don't know." Grandma fingered her thin hair and smoothed the blanket over her emaciated figure.

"I'm sure he'd love to talk to you again." Rachel waited, holding her breath. She wouldn't force Grandma to see Jim.

"On one condition." Grandma smiled wanly. "You have to help me with Gladys."

"You want to wear the wig?" Rachel slipped Gladys's hair off before Grandma could change her mind. "What should I do?"

"Here. Hand it to me." Grandma bent her head and pulled the wig on over her own hair. "Help me fix the back."

Rachel gently tugged the wig down, tucking in stray strands of gray hair. "Let me get your comb." She arranged the curls around Grandma's face, hiding the edges of the wig lining. Grinning widely, she provided her grandmother with a large hand mirror.

"Take a look!"

Rachel was amazed how the wig transformed her appearance. The blonde wig was beautifully curled, although it accented how thin and wrinkled Grandma's face had grown.

Grandma frowned into the mirror. "I don't know, Rachel," she said slowly, pulling at a curl. "I look like an old woman trying to be Marilyn Monroe."

"No, you don't. You look very pretty, Grandma."

Rachel glanced down the hall. "Can I go get Jim now?"

Grandma craned her neck for one last look, then took a deep breath. "Sure, why not?" She tossed her head, making the yellow curls bounce.

When Rachel went to get Jim, she was relieved to see his smile. He acted as if her outburst the week before had never happened. Rachel relaxed, grateful that he didn't hold grudges.

Entering the porch, Rachel watched Jim out of the corner of her eye. He blinked once, then twice. But he stepped forward eagerly and took Grandma's hand.

"Grandma P., I can't believe it's you!" He pulled the rocker close and folded his lanky frame down into it. "I thought Rachel had substituted a movie star in your bed!"

"Oh, phooey!" Grandma said, shaking her head. "You're just flattering an old woman."

Jim slapped his right hand over his heart, a horrified look on his face. "Would I do that?" he demanded of Rachel. "Would I?"

Rachel laughed. "Believe me, Grandma, he doesn't give compliments. At least not to me."

Grandma looked pleased and leaned back on her pillows. "Now, tell me all the news. I've been cooped up so long I feel out of touch. How is your band?"

"We're really improving," Jim said eagerly. "We

played at the eighth grade two-act drama intermission, then we volunteered to play for free at the mall one day. Some boat dealers had a display out there, and we played to attract a crowd."

Rachel started guiltily. She wasn't aware that Jim's group had played anywhere except in Steve's garage. Last year, she would have known every important thing happening in Jim's life.

Grandma clapped her hands. "I'm delighted, Jim, but not surprised. I've always known you were loaded with talent. Before long, you won't be playing for free—you mark my words."

"I know. We're booked for the seventh grade spring dance, and they're paying us. We won't get rich, but it's a start!"

Rachel stepped forward from the doorway. "That's great, Jim. I'm glad things are working out so well."

Rachel winced at the stilted sound of her words. She *was* happy for Jim, but she felt left out. She'd had no idea his group was so successful.

"What else have you been up to?" Grandma asked. "Or does your music group take all your free time?"

"I don't have much spare time now. Baseball practice started two weeks ago. We don't have our first game for three more weeks."

Rachel bit her lip, and spoke hesitantly. "That

reminds me. Isn't the Tigers' first baseball game this weekend? We haven't missed an opening game in five years."

To Rachel, this high school event marked the official beginning of spring. Loaded with hot dogs and Cokes, she and Jim sat in front row bleachers and screamed themselves hoarse.

Jim pushed his black hair back off his forehead. "Actually, that's what I came to ask you. A group of us are going to the game on Saturday. Steve's dad has a van and said he'd take us."

Rachel turned toward the window, her back to Jim. They'd always seen the Tigers' opening game together. Now he wanted to drag along a bunch of other people. They'd have no chance to talk privately. *Again.*

Opening her mouth to refuse the invitation, Rachel caught Grandma's warning glance. *"You have to learn to let go a little."* The remembered words echoed in her mind.

Rachel admitted that being with Jim, even with other kids around, would be better than not seeing him at all. She'd missed him.

She turned to Jim, breaking the uncomfortable silence. "I'd like to go. I'm sure that'll be fine with Mom. How about if I ask Kara to come too?"

"We could squeeze another body into the van. Sure, go ahead and ask her."

Grandma patted her blonde curls. "Since I don't want to make you girls jealous, I guess I'll stay home Saturday. But I want a full account of the game, play by play, when you get back."

Rachel nodded and laughed. "You've got it."

Monday and Tuesday raced by. Rachel felt as if a ten-ton weight had been lifted from her shoulders. It was great being friends with Jim again. She found herself looking forward to the baseball game that weekend.

But on Wednesday afternoon, Rachel's steps dragged as she walked the last block home. She hated Wednesdays—Grandma's days for chemotherapy. If it weren't for the treatment's side effects, Rachel could pretend that Grandma's cancer was just a bad dream.

Sure, where Grandma had been willowy before, she was now scrawny. She was more quiet and thoughtful, her book of poems and Bible never far from her hand. But these changes happened slowly, and Rachel could ignore them.

However, Wednesdays brought reality back, its pain a little sharper each time.

Coming around the tall honeysuckle hedge, Rachel was surprised to see the driveway empty. Marcia must be with another patient, she thought. That meant her mother was caring for Grandma alone.

Bracing herself, Rachel pushed open the front door.

Inside, she detected the soft murmur of voices at the back of the house. Rachel eased her stack of books onto the hall table, then headed down the hall to Grandma's bedroom.

Rachel paused outside the door, bending her lips into a stiff smile. On Wednesdays, being cheerful was almost impossible. Especially when she first saw Grandma, lying in bed and moaning.

Stepping through the door, she was jolted by the sight of Grandma sitting up in bed, holding a long-stemmed peachy orange rose. She didn't look sick at all! Her mother, relaxing in the rocker, turned and saw her.

"Hi, honey. How was your day?"

"Fine." Rachel smiled uncertainly. "You look great, Grandma. Didn't the treatment make you sick today?"

Grandma sniffed the rose before answering. "I didn't have chemotherapy today. Dr. Osborne did some tests last week; the results showed I don't need more treatments."

Rachel gasped. "That's wonderful! You really *are* getting better! I knew it!"

"Rachel—" her mother interrupted softly.

"I'm so glad you don't need more chemotherapy, Grandma. I hated the way it made you so sick. Now your hair will grow back in. I guess you won't need Gladys anymore!"

"Rachel!" Her mother's voice was sharp.

Rachel blinked, surprised.

Grandma intervened firmly. "Beverly, can you make me a cup of tea? I'm really thirsty."

"Are you sure?" Rachel's mother bit her lower lip.

"I'm sure."

Rachel looked from her mother to Grandma, puzzled at their brief exchange. But nothing else was said. Her mother patted Rachel on the shoulder, then left the room.

Suddenly, irrationally, Rachel was terrified. Grandma didn't need chemotherapy anymore, and her mother should have been ecstatic. Something was wrong, very wrong.

Grandma finally spoke, stroking Rachel's smooth hand with her bony one. "I didn't make things very clear, Rachel. I'm sorry. It's true—Dr. Osborne doesn't think I need to continue the chemotherapy. But it's not because I'm getting better."

"What are you saying?"

"The cancer is growing. The chemotherapy hasn't helped, so Dr. Osborne doesn't want me to suffer the side effects anymore."

Rachel swallowed twice before any words would come out. "Is he sure? Couldn't the tests be wrong?"

"I wish they were, Rachel. But I knew a long time ago that I wasn't getting any better. The tests just confirmed what I'd sensed for weeks."

Rachel blinked back the tears she felt forming. "How can you sound so calm?"

"Because I finally *feel* calm about it. I've had a lot of time to think, lying here day after day. But it took me weeks to accept the fact that I'm dying."

Rachel marveled at Grandma's matter-of-fact tone. She talked of dying as if it were no more than taking a trip.

"No one wants to die. I was angry at first and worried about being a financial burden on your parents. I wanted to live, but only if my life could be productive." She lay back on her pillows, her breath raspy. "When I realized I was getting worse, it was such a blow. I was even too sad to cry after a while."

Rachel nodded. "I know. Me too."

"But I know I've lived a rich, full life. Part of me will never die."

"What do you mean?"

"Part of me will always live as long as I have a child or grandchild on this earth. How lucky I've been to have you grow up in the same town with me! We've done things together that many people can't do because they live too far away."

Rachel breathed hard, overwhelmed at the turbulent feelings churning inside her. She wanted to tell Grandma how much she loved her, how much she enjoyed being with her. Baking, going for leisurely strolls, poring over old photo albums, picking strawberries, just talking . . . but she didn't trust her voice to say any of those things.

Just then, her mother arrived with the tea tray. She handed Grandma a cup of herbal tea and a soft cookie.

Rachel stood stiffly. "Um, I need to go change my clothes and study. I'll talk to you later, Grandma."

Grandma spoke quickly. "Are you all right, Rachel?"

"Sure. I'll come back after a while." She avoided her mother's eyes as she left the room.

Out in the kitchen, Rachel stared blankly out the window. Her mind refused to grasp the meaning of her grandmother's words.

Robotlike, she moved around the room, touching the cookie jar, the counter top, the bread box. Glancing at the key rack by the kitchen door, Rachel saw Grandma's house key hanging on the lower row of hooks. It was labeled with a little round cardboard tag.

On impulse she grabbed the key and dashed out the back door.

She jumped on her bike and pedaled furiously down the street. Looking neither right nor left, she followed the familiar route to Grandma's home. Two blocks from her destination, she blindly raced into an intersection.

An earsplitting screech of brakes brought her head up with a jerk. A green sports car swerved to avoid hitting her. A man in a business suit leaned out the driver's window, honking and shaking his fist.

Trembling, Rachel steered over to the curb. The sports car pulled around her and vroomed down the street.

A shudder ran through Rachel's body. Shaking herself slightly, she mounted her bike and pushed away from the curb. She stayed near the side of the street, concentrating on traffic lights and signs. Without further incidents, she arrived at Grandma's house ten minutes later.

The key fit the back door smoothly, and Rachel slipped into the empty house. The kitchen had an abandoned feel to it. She knew her mother aired the house regularly, but it still felt as if no human being had set foot there in months.

Rachel didn't know what she'd expected by coming to Grandma's house. Comfort, maybe. But she'd felt compelled to come—to curl up in the chairs where Grandma had sat, to gaze out the windows Grandma had looked through, to touch the things Grandma had touched.

Rachel felt the white kitchen curtains, running her finger along the double ruffle. Her hand brushed against something set on the window ledge. Glancing down, she saw the little bird she'd bought for Grandma the summer she was eight.

They had gone to Florida on vacation. In a souvenir shop, Rachel had bought the miniature pelican made from sea shells. She'd held the delicate figurine in her lap, wrapped in tissue paper, all the way home from Florida.

Rachel touched the smooth pink and beige shells. She realized now that the pelican was just a cheap souvenir, probably manufactured by the thousands for gullible tourists like herself. But Grandma had cherished it anyway, because Rachel had picked it out just for her.

Cradling the pelican in the palm of her hand, Rachel let the tears finally come.

9

The Rose

THE NEXT MORNING, as Rachel fixed a breakfast tray, her father ambled into the kitchen. "That for Grandma?" he asked.

Rachel nodded without glancing up. She'd tossed and turned most of the night, tying her sheets in knots, and didn't feel up to much conversation. She continued to fold the napkins and arrange the silverware.

Her dad reached around her to plug in the toaster. "I guess Grandma explained to you why Dr. Osborne stopped the chemotherapy. How do you feel?"

Rachel looked up, grateful that her father had asked. "Mostly I feel sad, but I'm not as angry as I was.

Talking with Grandma has helped me understand things better."

Dan Lincoln cleared his throat uncomfortably. "I wanted to talk to you about that. Grandma is suffering enough without having to deal with your confused feelings too. Your mother and I think it would be better if you didn't discuss Grandma's illness with her."

"I don't understand." Rachel slopped orange juice down the sides of the two glasses.

"That kind of talk is depressing, which is the last thing Grandma needs right now." He pushed two slices of raisin bread down in the toaster. "We're supposed to make Grandma as cheerful as possible."

Rachel mopped up the spilled juice. Maybe she'd been selfish, Rachel decided. Talking about her own feelings helped her, but was it too much to ask of Grandma? She had so much to deal with already.

Rachel balanced the tray on one arm. "I understand, Dad. I'll think of cheerful things to talk about."

Her dad turned to butter his toast. "Good girl, Rachel. I knew you'd understand."

Rachel padded down the short hallway to the porch bedroom. Grandma sat propped up in bed, surrounded by pillows, with her book of poetry open on her lap.

"Morning, Grandma." Rachel slid the breakfast tray onto the bedside table.

"Good morning, honey. Did you sleep well last night?"

Rachel was so tempted to lay her head in Grandma's lap and tell her no, she hadn't slept well at all. But remembering her dad's warning, she smiled deliberately.

"I slept like a rock. I was pretty tired." She handed Grandma a glass of orange juice. "It looks like nice weather outside today. I'll pick you a fresh rose after breakfast." Avoiding Grandma's eyes, she concentrated on her cold cereal.

"I was finally able to relax last night too." Grandma traced the squares of sunlight that made a checkerboard across her bed. "Now that I know I don't have much time left, I can accept it."

"You have *lots* of time left. Months and months. In fact, today I'm starting on a Christmas present for you that I want to make." Rachel wished her voice sounded less strained and more cheerful.

"Rachel, I thought you understood." Grandma chafed her gnarled hands together.

Rachel sighed and swallowed the mushy cereal in her mouth. "I do, Grandma. But it's depressing to talk about, don't you think?"

"Who have you been talking to? Your mom or your dad?"

"Dad." Rachel studied the multicolored striped carpet. "He says it's not fair to you to talk about your sickness. I'm supposed to cheer you up instead."

"I understand how your parents feel. But this illness is always on my mind, and I *need* to talk about it."

"Doesn't it upset you?"

"No, just the opposite." She leafed through the pages of her poetry book. "When I'm alone, though, there's a poem here that I love to read about a rose that grows up a wall."

"A rose?" Rachel was puzzled at the changed topic.

"Yes. A climbing rose is blooming beautifully as it climbs a shady wall." She turned two more pages and stopped. "Let me read you some of the poem, all right?"

"Sure." Rachel curled up in the rocker, hugging her knees tightly.

Grandma's voice started out strong. "The title is 'The Rose Beyond the Wall.' At first the climbing rose is watered by the dew as it blooms in the sunlight.

As it grew and blossomed fair and tall,
Slowly rising to loftier height,
It came to a crevice in the wall
Through which there shone a beam of light.

Onward it crept with added strength
With never a thought of fear or pride,
It followed the light through the crevice's length
And unfolded itself on the other side.

The light, the dew, the broadening view
Were found the same as they were before,
And it lost itself in beauties new,
Breathing its fragrance more and more.

"There's more, but this is exactly how I feel. There's life beyond the one we live now, Rachel. Just as the rose discovered on the other side of the wall." Grandma sank back, her breath coming in small wheezes and gasps.

Rachel gazed out the window at her mother's prize roses blooming along the back wall. Some climbed the fence like the rose in the poem.

"Do you really believe you'll live again, but in another place?"

"Absolutely, Rachel. For a fact."

Rachel rocked slowly, watching Grandma's tired face. She didn't know why, but somewhere, deep down inside, she believed what Grandma said. If the dead-looking rose bushes could blossom again, spring after spring, then surely Grandma would continue to live too.

"Can I get you something else to eat, Grandma? You haven't even tasted your egg." Rachel picked up the untouched tray.

"No, I'm not hungry this morning, but I'd love a fresh rose." Grandma handed Rachel the bud vase with the wilted flowers in it.

"I'll get one right away."

Grandma pulled the bedspread higher. "While you pick the roses, I think I'll take a little nap."

"Okay. I'll be back before I leave for school."

Rachel gazed for a moment at the tiny woman in the bed, then went to the kitchen. When she returned with the fresh roses, Grandma was asleep. She left the fragrant flowers on the bedside table, where she'd see them first thing.

THAT AFTERNOON when Rachel got home her mother was making a grocery list. Rachel changed her clothes, picked up her tray of shells to make barrettes, and joined Grandma on the porch. Five minutes later her mother left for the store.

As soon as the back door clicked shut, Grandma spoke. "Remember once before when I asked you to find homes for my house plants? Do you think you could do that now?"

Rachel drew in a sharp breath. She knew Grandma was making a perfectly reasonable request. But although Rachel was beginning to accept that Grandma was dying, the idea still hit her with terrible force.

"Rachel? Is that still too hard?"

Rachel studied Grandma's frail body propped up by pillows. Her wispy hair showed definite bald patches now, while her face grew more sunken each day.

Licking her lips, Rachel shook her head. "Just tell me where to deliver each plant. I'll make a list so I don't forget." With a sigh of resignation, she added, "I'll start taking the plants around tomorrow."

Grandma squeezed her hand before closing her dark-circled eyes. Rachel had an oddly relieved feeling, as if she had just passed an important test.

10

Blossom as the Rose

BY THE END of the week, Rachel had delivered eight plants to Grandma's friends. Each day after school she stopped for more plants, and as the week passed, being in Grandma's house grew easier. Rachel soon found it more comforting than disturbing to be surrounded by the things Grandma loved.

Delivering the philodendrons and ruffled African violets was easier than she'd expected. Grandma's friends were eager to hear about her. Rachel found it a relief to talk about Grandma's condition without having to guard her words.

Mrs. McCray, Grandma's best friend, begged to

visit Minna. Rachel hesitated, then explained that Grandma wanted to be remembered the way she'd been before her sickness. Rachel was surprised that she understood.

In fact, none of Grandma's friends acted offended that she didn't want them to visit. When they spoke of Grandma, some laughed. Others cried. All of them had been touched by Grandma. They were grateful to have something that had belonged to her.

Rachel arrived home late Thursday afternoon, after delivering the last plant, a wandering Jew, to Mr. Zimmerman. She took the stairs two at a time to get a necklace she was working on for her mom. She liked to work while she talked with Grandma after school.

Passing Brent's room, Rachel halted, surprised to see her older brother at home. Sweat ran down the sides of his beet-red face. His fists hoisted fifteen-pound dumbbells.

Rachel leaned against the door jamb. "How's Grandma today?" she asked. "And why aren't you at baseball practice?"

Grunting, Brent pulled the dumbbells to his chest. His biceps flexed like glossy boulders. "Coach's sick. Got the *measles* from one of his kids." He pumped the weights up and down. "I guess he's really sick."

"That's too bad. How's Grandma?"

"How would I know?" Brent examined a knotty knuckle. "I haven't seen her."

"Why not?" Rachel demanded, her voice sharp. "Was she asleep?"

"Drop the inquisition, Squirt." Brent swiped at his dripping face with the front of his T-shirt.

"You didn't even stop by her room, did you?" Rachel's voice climbed an octave. "You know all about the coach's measles, but you never go talk to Grandma, and she's living right in our house!"

"*Dying* in our house, you mean." Brent bent to untie his jogging shoes. "It isn't something I care to see."

"*Not something you care to see*! That's lousy! Grandma isn't a something! She's a person—with feelings!"

"Knock it off!" Brent jerked the window shade. It recoiled upward with a slapping noise and disappeared behind the curtain valance. "It wasn't *my* idea to have Grandma live here. So I don't have to visit someone who's dying."

Rachel stomped into his room. "Brent Lincoln, you're just a six-foot, two-inch *chicken*."

"Get out of here!"

"Sorry if the truth hurts." Rachel glared at her older brother. "It's no picnic for me either, sitting for hours every day, trying to think of things to talk about. But I do it because I love Grandma! I guess some people around here don't."

"That's a rotten thing to say. You don't know anything about it, so butt out."

Rachel stalked toward the door, then whirled around. "Don't you have any feelings at all?"

Brent's face turned to granite. "Yes, I have feelings." He twisted his shirt tail around his thumb. He paused, then added softly, "I do love Grandma."

"Then why don't you ever visit her?"

Brent strode to his dresser and picked up a carved wooden belt buckle. Rachel knew the buckle had been a gift from their grandfather when Brent was young. Brent handled the large buckle reverently, tracing the Indian head carved in the center.

"When you were still a baby, Grandpa took me everywhere with him. We fished and wandered trails while he told me old Indian legends. He was teaching me how to carve the afternoon before he died."

"I don't remember much about him," Rachel said, straddling his exercise bench.

"He and I were real close. Like you and Grandma, I guess. When he died, I thought I was going to die too." He laid the Indian buckle back on the piece of chamois. "So I don't want to be around Grandma now. Getting closer to her will make it harder when she dies."

Rachel picked pieces of chenille from Brent's bedspread. "I guess I understand. I hope Grandma does."

Without looking back, she went to her room, picked up the half-finished bead and rock necklace, and headed downstairs.

On the porch Rachel dropped into the rocker.

Trying to forget her fight with Brent, she explained to Grandma about delivering all the plants. She was glad the job was finished.

While arranging her beads and polished rocks on a tray, Rachel studied Grandma. Although the changes had been minimal from day to day, she could detect them now. Grandma's own gray hair was reduced to mere wisps, and lately she'd worn the pink knitted cap over her pale scalp.

"Anything else I can do for you at your house?" Rachel asked.

Grandma stroked the wood frame around Grandpa's picture. "Nothing really. I've left a will. Your parents will take care of selling the house later. But I *would* like to talk about my funeral."

Rachel jerked upright and braced herself. Although her heart pounded in her ears, she hoped she looked calm and unafraid.

"Your mother still won't let me talk, so I will tell you. I don't want my funeral to be sad." Grandma's smile stretched her parchment-thin skin over her cheek bones. "I want you to wear that bright red plaid dress of yours."

Rachel rubbed the polished agate she held in her hand. "Mom wouldn't let me in a million years. She'd say it didn't look respectful."

"Respectful?" Grandma snorted. "Dragging around in an ugly black dress shows more respect?" She lay back on her pillow, breathing hard. "I don't want a depressing funeral. I want lively organ music and singing. I want people to be happy that I'm not in pain anymore."

"You want us to remember you're blooming on the other side of the wall, is that it?"

"Exactly." Grandma stroked the worn cover of her Bible. "I know not everyone shares my beliefs, but I know what I know."

"I like your ideas, Grandma, but Mom will never agree." Rachel bit her lower lip. "When someone dies, you're supposed to wear dark colors and play dreary music. Otherwise, somebody might think you weren't sad at all."

"Not true! That isn't the only tradition." Grandma adjusted her pink hat to cover her ears. "My own grandmother was a school teacher at a small Indian school in Iowa. Their funeral customs made more sense to me."

"Like what?"

"Well, when a child died and was buried, the child's friends gathered at the burial site. Right over the grave, they played the dead child's favorite game. They were celebrating the child's new life."

"Was it the same when a grownup died?"

"Yes. If a woman died, for instance, her friends would gather and sit in a circle around the grave. They would talk about her while they did what that woman had enjoyed most—sewing, quilting, maybe singing."

"That sounds neat, but can you see Mom allow-ing anything like that?" Rachel shook her head.

"No, and I'm not asking for anything that drastic. But I want you to convince her not to have a sad funeral." Her eyes sparkled suddenly. "I know just how to set the right tone!"

"How?"

"Bring Gladys to my funeral! Who could be sad seeing the gorgeous smile you painted on her styrofoam head?"

Rachel glanced over at Gladys. "I guess she could come, as long as you don't mind her stealing the show."

"She'd add just the right touch."

Rachel straightened one of Gladys's blonde curls, shocked that she could make jokes with Grandma about her funeral. A quiet voice inside her head accused her of having no feelings.

But part of her was relieved. The thought of the funeral had terrified her. She remembered nothing about Grandpa's death, except that her mother had cried for days into a lacy handkerchief.

Talking about Grandma's funeral had drained part of the terror from it. For that, Rachel was grateful.

The next day at school, Rachel and Kara met at noon just inside the cafeteria door. As they inched down the lunch line, collecting a beef patty, cheese sandwich, pears, and milk, Rachel whispered to Kara about Grandma's wishes for her funeral.

They barricaded themselves behind stacks of books at a small table. Rachel opened her milk carton.

"It's funny, but it actually *helps* me to talk with Grandma about it."

"You're lucky." Kara pulled the cheese slice from her sandwich and tore it into strips. "Before my granddad died, he was in a nursing home for a year. We had to visit him every single Sunday afternoon, whether we wanted to or not."

"Doesn't sound like you liked it much."

"I hated it. He got mean and crabby. He'd say things like 'I know you'll be glad when I die.' Lots of times he accused the nurses of poisoning him or trying to suffocate him."

"That's horrible! I bet he wouldn't have acted that way if he'd lived with your family instead of at a nursing home. I know Grandma doesn't think we'll be happier when she's gone."

"Like I said, your family's lucky." Kara studied her beef patty, then turned it over and covered it with ketchup.

"Do you wish your granddad could have stayed with you?"

"No, not in a million years. Not all old people are like your grandmother, you know. My granddad would have made us miserable if he'd stayed with us. It was bad enough seeing him throw tantrums on Sunday afternoons."

"What happened when he threw tantrums?"

"My parents would paste on these fake smiles for the nurses. They ignored what Granddad said and pretended that everything was fine." She popped the rolled strip of cheese into her mouth.

"My mom keeps pretending too." Rachel carved a face in her pear half. "She won't let Grandma talk about the cancer or the funeral or anything. That makes Grandma sad."

"My granddad didn't seem sad. He just got madder until the day he died. By that time he was swearing at everybody who came in the room. He got really weak, but he was strong enough to cuss and throw his lunch tray at the nurses."

"He threw his food? Why?"

"I don't know. But I *do* know one thing. Nobody actually said so, but my whole family was relieved when he finally died." Kara glanced up. "You'll probably think I'm rotten, but I was glad not to have to visit him anymore."

Rachel remembered all the long talks she and Grandma had had the last few weeks. They were special times.

Maybe missing someone you loved after she had died wasn't the worst thing that could happen. It had to be better than feeling like Kara did. Rachel finished her meal in silence, intent on this new idea.

❦

THAT NIGHT at home Rachel decided a root beer float was in order to give her novel a little zip. Kara had lent her *Love at Summer Camp*, and Rachel was having a tough time keeping her mind on the story. Maybe a float would help.

She stopped at the porch door on the way to the kitchen. "Want a root beer float, Grandma? I'm making one for me."

Her grandmother sat propped in bed, a pencil in her hand. "Now that you mention it, a glass of plain root beer sounds good. Your mother and Marcia Carlson mean well, but I'm sick of milk and eggnog."

Rachel couldn't blame her one bit. "I'll be right back with a glass." Minutes later she returned with her float and Grandma's glass of root beer. "What's that you're working on?"

Grandma handed the notepad to Rachel. "I decided I was asking a lot of you earlier. It's not up to you to give Beverly instructions about my funeral."

"Then you've talked to Mom about it?" Rachel scanned Grandma's list.

"Not yet. I haven't finished my list. I write so slow, and my writing isn't so good anymore."

"I could jot things down for you." Rachel chipped at a hard chunk of vanilla ice cream in her float. "What should I write?"

Even as she spoke, Rachel was inwardly horrified at her matter-of-fact tone of voice. She could be writing down a grocery list instead of funeral arrangements.

"What's the matter?" Grandma asked. "Are you sure you don't mind doing this?"

"No, but . . . it sounds so cold and unfeeling, helping to plan your funeral."

"A few months ago I wouldn't have believed it was possible either. But I've accepted what's happening, and I want to help you accept it too."

"Sometimes it still doesn't seem real." Rachel felt tears welling up in her eyes and bent over her root beer float. Pretending to drink, she waited until the sharp pain behind her eyes subsided. "But I think I'm learning to accept it, at least a little bit."

"Good, then write this down." Grandma spoke briskly. "I want to be buried in my dusty rose knit dress, the one with the tiny pearl buttons. I want to wear the heart-shaped locket that's in my jewelry box. It has your grandfather's and Beverly's pictures in it."

As Rachel wrote, she had the strangest sensation of being a mere onlooker in the room. What she was doing didn't seem real. Shaking herself, she asked, "What else?"

Grandma rubbed the top of her scalp. "I do appreciate Gladys, really I do, but I don't want to be buried wearing a wig. Since I'm so skinny now, and bald too, I want a closed casket. *No one* at the funeral is to see me." She leaned over the list. "Maybe you should underline that part. I don't want any misunderstanding."

Rachel dutifully underlined *closed casket*. "What else?"

"There's a verse in Isaiah that I want printed on

the little remembrance cards they hand out before funerals. It says: 'The wilderness and the solitary place shall be glad for them; and the desert shall rejoice, and blossom as the rose.' "

Rachel wrote rapidly. "I've got it. Anything else?"

Grandma lay back, breathing rapidly. "I'll have to give you the other instructions later. I seem to have run out of steam."

"That's okay. Where do you want this list kept?"

"Hide it somewhere. It will upset Beverly to know we've discussed this." Grandma closed her eyes, and the web of tired lines in her forehead eased a bit.

Rachel lifted a corner of the mattress and slipped the half-finished list under it. Straightening, she whispered, "If you need anything, holler. You can interrupt *Love at Summer Camp* anytime you want."

Grandma made no comment, but continued to lie still with her eyes closed. Suddenly alarmed, Rachel leaned closer. She strained to hear some reassuring sound. At last she detected a soft, wheezy sigh. She leaned weakly against the wall, her quivering knees threatening to buckle.

For one horrid moment, Rachel'd thought . . . But no. It couldn't be time yet.

Her heart's pounding gradually slowed to its regular rhythm. With a last swallow of flat root beer, Rachel tiptoed off down the hall.

11

"Be With Me"

DURING THE NEXT two weeks Rachel watched in silence as Grandma grew worse. She responded more slowly. During their conversations, Grandma was apt to drift off to sleep in the middle of a sentence.

When she was awake, Grandma directed Rachel to make more lists for her. She said she was too tired to do anything but think, and Rachel would have to be her hands for her.

So Rachel made detailed lists of personal possessions for Grandma's different nieces and nephews. At the end of three weeks, Rachel had written plans for the sharing of Grandma's furniture, jewelry, old dishes, and photographs.

One Wednesday afternoon late in May, Rachel was spraying her dresser with lemon polish when she heard the crunch of gravel outside. She pressed her nose against the dusty window screen and looked down.

Below, Nurse Carlson rolled down her car window, removed her sunglasses, and stepped out.

Rachel jumped back from the baggy screen, changed her T-shirt, and yanked a brush through her hair. She'd missed Marcia's last three visits, and there were some questions she wanted to ask her. Rachel'd never had the nerve to call Marcia at work, although she'd memorized her phone number.

Downstairs, Rachel peeked into Grandma's room, but she lay asleep, softly snoring. She tiptoed down the hall to the kitchen, where her mom and Marcia were already sipping from tall glasses of iced tea.

Marcia pointed to a blue mimeographed paper. "These foods will be all she can handle now. Plus anything that can be reduced to a liquid—like ice cream or gelatin."

Tripping, Rachel's elbow whacked the refrigerator. She knocked two ladybug magnets to the floor.

Marcia whirled around. "Rachel! I've missed talking with you the last few weeks."

Rachel felt suddenly shy. Staring at her torn fingernail, she said, "I was at school."

"That's why I came later today." She wiped beads of sweat from her upper lip and hooked her long hair behind her ears. "I thought you might have some questions."

"Um, not really." She'd promised her parents not to talk to Grandma about the cancer, so she couldn't ask her questions without her mom guessing the truth.

Silence settled over the kitchen like a damp cloth. Rachel wished she hadn't come downstairs after all.

"Minna is sleeping right now," Marcia said. "Since it's such a gorgeous day, would you like to walk around the block with me? I could use some exercise."

"Um, sure." Rachel glanced at her mom from underneath her eyelashes. She'd prefer going with Marcia alone, but she didn't want her mother to feel left out. "Mom, do you want to come with us?"

"No thanks, honey." Her mother fished a limp lemon slice out of the dripping tea glass. "I don't like to leave Grandma alone these days, even for a little while."

"We won't be gone long," Marcia said. "When Minna wakes up, tell her I'll be right back."

Outside, Rachel breathed deeply, feeling her lungs expand. The atmosphere in the kitchen had been suffocating. But out in the brilliant May sunshine, words came more easily.

"How have you been?" Marcia swung her arms and matched her steps to Rachel's.

"Okay, most of the time." Rachel stepped over a

crack in the sidewalk and stopped. Staring down, she watched two red ants drag a cricket leg across the cement. "Grandma's getting worse, isn't she?"

"What makes you ask that?"

"Well, she looks worse. Her hair is all gone now, and I bet she doesn't even weigh a hundred pounds anymore." She paused, chewing her bottom lip. "She talks about her funeral. She asked me to write down the dress she wants to be buried in."

"Does it bother you a lot, hearing her talk this way?"

"It's funny, but for some reason, it's easier than *not* talking about it. And Grandma feels better when everything is written down."

Marcia nodded thoughtfully. Taking Rachel's hand, she guided her into an ice cream store on Center Street, where she ordered two chocolate dipped cones. Marcia handed one to Rachel, grabbed a paper napkin, and they left the store.

Rachel sensed that Marcia was stalling for time, choosing her words.

Back outside, they crossed the street to the Lions Midtown Park. Rachel chipped the chocolate glaze from her cone, letting it melt in her mouth.

The small park was nearly deserted. Rachel and Marcia straddled the little kids' red-and-blue horse swings, gliding easily as they licked their drippy cones.

Wiping at the vanilla ice cream running down her hand, Marcia finally spoke. "I'm glad Minna has you to confide in, but do you feel it's too much for you to handle?"

Rachel loosened a blue paint chip from her horse's nose. "At first it was awful when Grandma talked about dying. I didn't want to listen." She gouged a hole with her tennis shoe in the sand below her. "I think she kept talking about it to help me understand what was happening."

"Has talking helped you?"

Rachel leaned back, staring up into the oak trees overhead, concentrating on the dancing patterns of the leaves. "It's helped some. But I'm not ready to lose her yet."

"I know. But I'm glad for your sake and Minna's, that you're able to listen to her."

"Then why won't Mom and Dad talk honestly with Grandma? They told me to stop her from talking about her cancer—or death. They say it's wrong. And Brent—Brent won't even *see* her. He pretends nothing is happening at all!"

Marcia flexed her fingers. Her engagement ring glittered in the sun. "How people handle illness depends a lot on how they were raised. *Many* people cannot talk about death. Sometimes it's too frightening, or makes them too uncomfortable. They're perfectly entitled to these feelings."

"Mom says we're just supposed to say cheerful things."

"I understand how your mother feels. But your

grandmother has a great faith and isn't afraid of dying. She talks a lot about wanting to help you through this very hard time."

Rachel bent over her cone, blinking rapidly. It was just like Grandma to worry about *other* people when she was so sick.

She cleared her throat. "How long before Grandma dies?"

"If I knew that, I'd tell you, Rachel. But no one knows." Marcia crunched into her sugary cone. "I *can* give you some idea of what to expect in the next weeks."

Rachel braced herself. No longer hungry, she tossed the rest of her cone in a nearby metal trash can. Marcia joined her, and together they strolled past the deserted merry-go-round, jungle gym, and teeter-totters.

"Her diet has changed, as you probably heard me tell your mother. Minna's body functions are slowing down, including some of her senses. Have you noticed that she's slower to respond to you?"

"Yes. Sometimes her words are garbled. That frustrates her when she's trying to tell me something."

"That will happen more often. She will gradually sleep more hours out of each day." Marcia bent to pick three blue violets from the base of an oak tree. "It will become harder for her to see well, to speak, and to move. She will almost appear to be in a coma sometimes."

"Appear to be?"

"Although she won't be able to respond sometimes, she'll still be able to hear you. Quite often hearing is the last sense a person keeps. So it's very important that you keep talking to her."

"What about?" Rachel wasn't sure she could carry on a one-sided converation.

"Tell her about your school day, read to her, things like that." She stopped at the edge of the park and knelt in front of Rachel. "I know it's a lot to ask. I've asked your parents to treat Minna this way too. Do you think you can do it?"

"It'll be hard when she can't answer me," Rachel said haltingly. She stared at the delicate violets Marcia handed her. "But I can talk to her and read to her, or just sit with her. I can do that."

Marcia squeezed her hand. "Your grandmother is very lucky to have you." Standing, she headed back across the street. "We should get back now. Minna might be awake, and I look forward to my visits with her."

Rachel slipped off the curb with a jolt. "You look forward to visiting dying people?" she asked in surprise.

"Frankly, I don't enjoy all my patients. Not all terminally ill people are like Minna. But with her, sometimes I don't know who's doing the cheering up. Often *I'm* the one who comes away feeling, well, more refreshed."

Rachel nodded. She knew exactly what Marcia meant.

During the next two weeks, Rachel tried not to let Grandma know she was keeping a close eye on her. A sense of dread filled her as she spotted the signs Marcia mentioned. With a heavy sinking feeling, she watched Grandma withdraw from her.

Grandma began to sleep a lot more, sometimes drifting off right in the middle of a sentence. Those times, Rachel wasn't sure if she was really asleep or just not strong enough to talk anymore. Or, like Marcia said, some of the drowsiness could be from the pain medication she received.

Whatever the reason, Rachel would assume Grandma could hear her. She'd continue talking, although she felt rather foolish.

With trouble swallowing, Grandma ate less, growing thinner and ashen-colored. She became smaller, quieter, and more remote each day.

One day after school, Rachel spotted Jim on the way out the front door and ran to catch up with him. It was a sparkling clean spring day, with a gentle breeze, just perfect for a bike ride out to Vandermeer's Pond. Rachel suddenly felt a need to be with a friend her own age, outside in the fresh air.

"How about it, Jim?" she asked, shifting her books to her other arm. "Spring's almost gone, and we haven't been out there once yet!"

"Well, I already made some plans—"

Rachel shook her finger at him. "Haven't you heard that all work and no play makes Jim a dull boy? Your music group can get along without a drummer for one afternoon, can't they?"

"I wasn't going to—" Jim began.

He was interrupted as Amy Greer flounced through the double doors. "Oh, there you are!" She hooked her hand through Jim's arm. "I'm so glad you can help me with my science report at the library this afternoon." Amy noticed Rachel for the first time. "Oh, hi, Rachel."

"Hi, Amy." Rachel forced her frozen lips into a small smile. "I'd better get going. Have a good time." She hurried away, the knife in her chest stabbing deeper with each step.

When was she ever going to learn?

She shook her head angrily until stringy strands of hair stung her eyes. Jim had shown her all year that he had outgrown their childhood friendship. As often as he had rejected her lately, it shouldn't hurt so much this time.

But it did.

She clenched her jaw until her teeth ached. She was *not* going to cry. She wouldn't!

Jogging all the way home, she pushed open the front door. Instinctively, she gravitated toward her grandmother's room. Grandma would understand about Jim.

Grandma sat propped up in bed, holding a delicate purple iris. "Hi, honey. Look what your mother just brought me." Her trembling hand made the paper-thin petals quiver.

"I love how irises smell." Rachel leaned over the bed and sniffed. "How do you feel today?"

"Kind of weak." Her eyes had trouble focusing on Rachel's face. "How . . . are you today?"

Remembering Marcia's advice, Rachel launched into a dramatic account of her day, embellishing where necessary to make a more exciting story. Her reward was a small smile that twitched at the corners of Grandma's lips.

". . . and this afternoon Sally Woods broke the glass on the science aquarium. Two snakes got loose and you should have seen all the screaming girls standing on their desks!" Rachel grinned at the memory of Kara holding her teen romance high above her head, as if the snakes would devour it.

"Sounds funny." Grandma closed her eyes for a moment, then slowly opened them again. "But when you came home . . . you looked . . ." She paused again, gasping. ". . . upset."

A picture of Amy hanging on Jim's arm flooded her mind. "It's nothing much. I invited Jim to go biking to the pond with me." Rachel glanced at her grandfather's framed photo on the bedside table. "But Jim already had plans with—"

She stopped abruptly, seeing Grandma's eyes were closed again. Was she taking a nap? Rachel wished she could tell. Marcia had said Grandma could have her eyes closed and not respond, but still be awake.

Rachel stared at Grandma's fingers. The nail beds were gray. "He'd already made plans with Amy Greer," she went on. "You would have been pleased with me, though, Grandma. I didn't throw a fit or anything. I think I even told them to have a good time."

Rachel paused, studying her grandmother's face. No eyelid flickered. No facial muscle twitched. There was no movement at all. Rachel decided she really must be asleep this time.

Placing the yellow-centered blue iris in the vase on the night table, Rachel tiptoed to the door. Just as she reached the doorway, a whispery voice floated to her.

"Be . . . with me."

Whirling around, Rachel saw Grandma lying in the exact same position, with her eyes closed. She hurried back to the bed and took her grandmother's withered hand in her own.

"I'm sorry, Grandma. I thought you were asleep." She kicked off her shoes, sat on the bed, and tucked one foot under her. "I know you're too tired to talk right now. That's okay." Her glance rested on the books beside the bed. "How about if I read for a while?"

There was no response.

Rachel reached for the book of poems anyway. She read short poems and longer verses, one after another. Some made her sad, like "Holding Your Hand" and "When Winter Comes."

But others, like "Experience" and "An Evening Hope," brought her peace, and she read them avidly. She began to understand Grandma's love for poetry.

The satiny pages whispered as she turned them. Not once did she see any response on her grandmother's face. When she was tempted to quit, Rachel remembered Grandma's words: "Be with me." And so she read on.

When the hickories in the backyard blocked the setting sun, shadows filled the porch. The words of the poems blurred, and Rachel finally closed the book. Bending over, her lips brushed Grandma's cheek.

Rachel leaned over to place the book on the night stand. The book slipped, knocking against the table. Grandpa Potter's framed picture fell to the floor with a deafening crash.

Rachel gasped and held her breath. But Grandma continued to lie still, as if the noise had happened in a vacuum.

Rachel retrieved the picture from where it had landed face down. Turning it over, she spotted a thin crack that ran from one side of the glass up to the opposite corner. She slid her finger along the crack. The break was hardly noticeable as it ran across Grandpa's mustache and up through his cheek.

Rachel felt the way her grandfather looked. She suspected that if anyone looked close enough, he'd also find she had a big crack running through her.

Sighing, Rachel replaced the photo on the stand and left.

THE NEXT DAYS blended together in a haze. The house was too quiet: Rachel's mother and dad spoke in whispers and stopped talking when Rachel entered the room.

Grandma lay quietly in bed. It was usually impossible to tell when she slept and when she was awake. But Rachel kept her afternoon ritual, telling Grandma about her day, then reading to her for an hour. Usually Grandma tried to speak once during that time, but Rachel could rarely decipher the words.

That was the hardest part.

ONE FRIDAY afternoon Rachel bounded down the school steps, anxious to get home. She and Kara were going on a bike hike after she spent her time with Grandma. They walked together as far as Elm, then split to go their separate ways.

Rachel raced the last three blocks home. She planned to change into cut-offs and sandals, grab some apples and cookies, and meet Kara in an hour. The day was perfect to be outside having fun.

Stepping into the front hall, she set her English book on the bottom step and tiptoed down the hall toward the porch. In the doorway she stopped as abruptly as if she'd slammed into a brick wall.

Grandma's bed was empty!

Rachel stumbled into the room, bewildered. No! It couldn't be true! Where was Grandma?

She whirled around and raced to the living room. Her father stood near the book shelves, staring at the rows of titles. Rachel was surprised to see him home so early. When he noticed her, he walked toward her and wrapped his arms around her without a word.

"I didn't hear you come in." He stroked her hair awkwardly. "I'm sorry, Rachel. I'm so sorry."

Rachel felt as if she couldn't breathe. Pulling back, she demanded, "Is Grandma at the hospital? Did she get worse?"

When her dad avoided looking at her, she knew the truth. She'd really known the minute she saw the empty bed. Taking a deep breath, she asked, "When?"

"After lunch, about two o'clock. Beverly found Grandma when she brought her some hot milk. She'd died in her sleep."

For a moment, Rachel had forgotten all about her mother. "Where is Mom? How is she?"

"She's resting now. Dr. Osborne gave her something to help her sleep. In fact, I should go check on her now. Are you all right?"

Rachel nodded, knowing that's what he expected. After her father left the room, she stumbled like a sleepwalker back to the porch.

She groped her way to the empty bed, seeing the room through a watery haze. She gently touched the rumpled pillow. Two gray hairs still lay there.

Rachel pulled the bedspread off the bed, dragging it over to the rocker. Collapsing into the chair, she wrapped the bedspread around her shoulders and rocked slowly back and forth.

Without making a sound, she stared at the vase on the night table and the single red rose it held.

12

The Rose Beyond the Wall

THE NEXT TWO DAYS blurred together for Rachel. Nothing seemed real nor could penetrate her shell to actually touch her. Her senses were numb as she moved through the days. Except for sudden, sharp times of crying, she was calm.

At least on the surface.

She'd been relieved when she discovered Grandma had given Marcia her lists before she died. Marcia herself had told Rachel's parents of Grandma's wishes for her funeral.

The red spiral notebook of lists had also made it easier when Pastor Rollins talked to them about the funeral. Rachel was satisfied that it would be as much like Grandma wanted as possible.

After the funeral, Rachel could only remember certain scenes. It was like a photo album in her mind, with specific memories captured on celluloid.

In one photograph, Jim stood with his parents. He wore a blue suit with hems and cuffs an inch too short.

In another picture, Marcia waited at the back of the church. Her head was bent, and her long hair hid her face. Rachel had wanted to stop and speak to her, but she wasn't sure it was the proper thing to do. So she'd continued down the aisle beside Brent, behind her mom and dad.

Back at the house, Rachel helped her mother serve the sliced ham and potato salad and rolls and pies that neighbors had brought the day before. Like someone in a trance, she answered her aunts' and uncles' questions about school.

Although outwardly calm as she passed among the chattering groups of people, Rachel had an almost irresistible urge to scream at them.

How could they be gossiping and even laughing at a time like this? How could the world go on when something so terrible had just happened?

And Rachel wondered how they could stand to eat. She couldn't even think about food. Yet the platters of meat and bowls of salad in the kitchen disappeared while the wastebasket filled with used paper plates and cups.

As she collected dirty glasses in the living room, Rachel smiled and nodded at Grandma's friends, but barely heard what they said. Their words were garbled and distorted, as if she were hearing them from under water.

She wanted desperately to go to her room and be alone. It was wrong for Grandma's relatives and friends to eat and laugh as if it were just another day.

They actually seemed to be *enjoying* themselves.

Then she recalled Grandma talking about her great-great-grandmother at the Indian school. There, friends had gathered at the fresh graves to sing or sew or play a game.

Remembering, Rachel had to correct herself. The laughing relatives might bother Rachel, but she knew it would have pleased Grandma.

The next week passed quickly, although each individual day seemed twice as long as usual. Most of the time Rachel felt weighed down, as if a ten-ton truck were parked on her chest. It made it hard to be enthusiastic about anything.

At school, with only one week of classes left, her friends busily made plans for the summer. Rachel listened to the talk about camp and trips to the mountains and summer jobs, but had little to add. Nothing sounded like any fun.

She'd always spent much of her vacation time at Grandma's house. This year there would be a lot of empty hours to fill.

Although Kara had come by often, Rachel knew she was being lousy company. She felt compelled to constantly talk about Grandma—the things Grandma had said, the things they'd done together, the last hard months of knowing she was dying. Only by reliving it could she sort it out in her mind.

Rachel knew Kara was sick of hearing about it over and over, and she didn't blame her. So Rachel gradually spent more time by herself.

One day when she came home from school, her mother was struggling to fold up Grandma's rollaway bed. With the bedside table gone and Gladys in her round box, the bedroom looked more like the old porch.

Her mom's exercise bicycle stood in one corner, next to a stack of gardening magazines. The wicker furniture was back in place, as well as the extra record player.

"Sure looks strange in here now," Rachel said, helping her mother hook the metal bars that held the bed together. "So empty."

"I know, honey." Her mother leaned over to lift Grandma's Bible and poetry book from the box by the door. "Grandma wanted you to have these things."

Rachel stared at the books for a long moment before touching them. They were probably some of the last things Grandma had touched. The volumes meant a lot to her, but it was too painful to read them now.

"Thanks, Mom." She cradled the books in her arms. "It hurts to think this is all we have left of Grandma."

"Yes, it does. Sorting through her belongings over at the house was very hard." Her mom perched on the bike seat. "At least I like the family who bought her house."

"Me too—I hate the idea of strangers living there. But you know, I think Grandma would be happy that a family with little kids bought her house."

"That's true. She always loved the sound of children's voices." Rachel's mother jumped down from the exercise bike suddenly and returned to working on the room.

Rachel leaned against the door frame and watched for a minute. She would have helped put Grandma's things away, but most of the work was already done.

Her mom had said very little about Grandma's death so far, and Rachel sensed that she still preferred to keep her feelings to herself. Rachel guessed she understood—Marcia had said everyone dealt with death in his own way. But sometimes it made things kind of lonely.

On the last day of school, the sun floated in a brilliant blue sky. Early that morning Rachel leaned on her bedroom windowsill as she stared out through the leafy tree tops. In spite of the last weeks, she felt her spirits rise. It was going to be a beautiful day—just the kind she loved.

She chewed on a granola bar as she packed her sack lunch for the traditional "last day of school" picnic. The teachers furnished pop and ice cream, and the students ate outside under the ancient spreading oaks. It was the perfect kickoff for summer.

At noon Rachel and Kara brushed aside a layer of old crushed acorns to make a comfortable spot to eat their sandwiches. They were waiting until the crowd at the main doors thinned out before standing in line for drinks and ice cream.

Kara scrubbed at the blob of ketchup she'd squirted onto her plaid blouse. "I can't wait until two o'clock for summer to officially begin. I bought eight new romances, and I'm going to read a new book every day until my eyes give out." She sighed blissfully. "What are you going to do?"

Rachel shrugged and bit into her meat loaf sandwich. "I haven't made any plans yet."

"Good," said a voice behind her.

Rachel twisted around to look over her shoulder. "Hi, Jim. Why's it good that I don't have any plans?"

Jim dropped down on the grass beside Rachel and Kara. "Because I thought we could bike out to Vandermeer's Pond this afternoon. I got some fresh bait last night."

"I'd love to." She paused, remembering all the times she'd wanted to make plans with Jim. Trying to make her voice light, she asked, "Who else is coming?"

"Nobody." Jim stole a handful of her potato chips and stuffed them into his mouth. "You know we always do something on the last day of school—just the two of us."

Rachel grinned suddenly. "How could I have forgotten? What time should we go?"

"We're free from this prison at two. I'll give you half an hour to get home, change, grab your fishing rod and some food. How's two-thirty?"

"Great. I'll raid the cookie jar for you since you're bringing extra bait for me." Rachel snatched back her potato chip bag.

Jim unfolded his long legs accordian-style and rose to his feet. "See you later, then." He saluted jauntily and ambled away.

Rachel grinned at Kara. "I guess I have some plans after all." She watched Jim zigzag through the crowd. "Just like old times."

As soon as she received her final report card at two, Rachel sped out of the building without looking back. Although she had plenty of time, she wouldn't risk being late. Like a tin soldier, she swung her arms as she marched briskly toward home.

She couldn't believe it. Jim wanted to be with her, just the two of them. Grandma had been right about "letting go" of him. Rachel knew now she had nearly choked the friendship to death.

She had an overwhelming desire to tell Grandma all about it.

The words formed clearly in her mind. "Grandma, you were right about Jim. I took your advice, and he finally asked me to go biking this afternoon. I guess I do hold on to people too tight. But I'm learning."

At home Rachel left a note for her mother in the kitchen, then hurried down the hall. Passing the porch, she halted. It still took a split-second shock to remember Grandma wasn't out there on the porch anymore.

Seeing the tennis rackets, exercise bike, and wicker furniture, Rachel had an odd feeling that the past months had been a bad dream. Her memories were hazy sometimes, almost as if Grandma had never been there.

Shaking her head, she turned toward the stairs and took them two at a time. Jim would be ready in fifteen minutes; she didn't want to be late. She quickly changed into grubby old cut-off jeans and a faded sweatshirt.

Turning to leave, she glanced at her dresser. Grandma's Bible and book of poems lay in the exact spot where Rachel had first placed them.

Without understanding why, she finally felt able

to touch the books Grandma had prized so highly. Kneeling on the floor with the poem book, Rachel carefully turned the pages. She recognized many of the verses she'd read to Grandma during the last days of her life.

On the last page was a photograph of a rose climbing a garden wall. She recalled the day Grandma had talked about "blooming" in another life.

That day Grandma had read some verses from this poem. The poet had written how a rose had climbed a shady wall and discovered a crevice. Following a beam of light through this crack, the rose unfolded itself on the other side. The light and the view on the other side of the wall were found the same as they were before.

Rachel leaned back against her bed, wishing Grandma could come back and reassure her that there was, indeed, light on the other side. She wanted to be sure. Sighing, Rachel glanced at the poem. She read silently the verses Grandma had shared.

She was surprised, however, to find the poem had two more verses. As she read aloud, she could almost hear her grandmother's voice.

Shall claim of death cause us to grieve
And make our courage faint and fall?
Nay! Let us faith and hope receive—
The rose still grows beyond the wall,

Scattering fragrance far and wide
Just as it did in days of yore,
Just as it did on the other side,
Just as it will forevermore.

Tracing the rose petals with her finger, Rachel understood that *this* was Grandma's message of hope for her.

Rachel returned the book to her dresser, then picked up her paper sack full of oatmeal cookies. Feeling the warmth of the sun's rays that streamed through her bedroom window, she paused.

"Keep blooming, Grandma," she whispered.

With a new bounce in her step, she smiled and left the room.

THE ROSE BEYOND THE WALL

Near shady wall a rose once grew,
Budded and blossomed in God's free light,
Watered and fed by morning dew,
Shedding its sweetness day and night.

As it grew and blossomed fair and tall,
Slowly rising to loftier height,
It came to a crevice in the wall
Through which there shone a beam of light.

Onward it crept with added strength
With never a thought of fear or pride,
It followed the light through the crevice's length
And unfolded itself on the other side.

The light, the dew, the broadening view
Were found the same as they were before,
And it lost itself in beauties new,
Breathing its fragrance more and more.

Shall claim of death cause us to grieve
And make our courage faint and fall?
Nay! Let us faith and hope receive—
The rose still grows beyond the wall,

Scattering fragrance far and wide
Just as it did in days of yore,
Just as it did on the other side,
Just as it will forevermore.

(From the writings of A. L. Frink)